The Gamble

Samantha Alexander lives in Lincolnshire with a variety of animals and a schedule almost as busy and exciting as her plots! She writes a number of columns for newspapers and magazines, is a teen-age agony aunt for Radio Leeds and in her spare time she regularly competes in show-jumping, dressage and eventing.

HOLLYWELL STABLES

The Gamble
2

Samantha Alexander

**MACMILLAN
CHILDREN'S BOOKS**

First published 1995 by Macmillan Children's Books

a division of Macmillan Publishers Ltd
25 Eccleston Place, London SW1W 9NF
and Basingstoke

Associated companies throughout the world

ISBN 0 330 33685 1

3 5 7 9 8 6 4

A CIP catalogue record for this book is available from
the British Library.

Phototypeset by Intype, London
Printed and bound in Great Britain by
Mackays of Chatham PLC, Chatham, Kent

Chapter One

"It's worked!" my brother bawled out, rushing up our muddy field in overlarge wellies and clutching a piece of paper which he was waving frantically in the air.

At that moment I could have gladly throttled him. He must know by now not to wave things in the air around horses; especially horses like Colorado who were half thoroughbred/half Mustang and likely to go off like a firework at the slightest noise.

I was just coming into a row of jumps which Ross called a grid and was designed to improve a horse's confidence but Colorado's concentration was now shot to pieces.

"Mel – Wait!" Ross yelled, running faster, up to his knees in mud and looking more excited than I'd ever seen him. I reined in Colorado and wondered what on earth was going on.

"It's worked," he gasped, finally reaching me, looking beetroot in the face and in need of resuscitation.

"What?" I yelled back. "Ross, what are you talking about?"

"It's Rocky," he said. "He's coming, he's coming to our village hall."

It was all of thirty seconds before what Ross was telling me finally sunk in. I wanted to scream Yippee! at the top of my voice, but I couldn't because I was on top of Colorado so I just sat there grinning from ear to ear like a pools' winner.

It was unbelievable. It was incredible. It was like a dream come true.

"I don't believe it," I croaked. "Ross, are you sure you've got it right?"

But there was no mistaking the gold-embossed letter heading and the very special signature at the bottom of the letter.

In a complete daze I put Colorado in his stable and then sat down in our tack room on a wooden chest marked "horse rugs". I read the letter fifty times over but it still wouldn't sink in.

Ross was pacing up and down running his hand through his jet black hair looking as if he was about to explode with excitement.

"Have you any idea how big this could be?" he kept saying over and over again.

The letter was from the personal manager of one of the most famous rock stars in the world. He'd had more number ones than I could remember and it was even rumoured that he was a close friend of the Princess of Wales. He was one of the biggest names in music and he was coming to our village hall!

Ages and ages ago Ross had written to him explaining about Hollywell Stables – our sanctuary for horses and ponies – how we rescued horses in desperate need and how we needed more money to continue our work. We had asked him if on his next tour to England he could possibly do a concert in our village hall with the proceeds going to Hollywell Stables. It was a long-shot but we had heard of other famous bands doing similar things for charity so it was not totally out of the ordinary. There was a chance, even if it was a very small one.

But when we didn't receive an answer straight away we had given up on the idea. Even my little sister Katie had stopped talking about it.

The letter was like a bolt out of the blue.

"I don't believe it," Katie yelled out in a state of shock when she read the letter for the first time. Her eyes bulged out of their sockets and her face went as brick-red as her special Hollywell Stables sweatshirt.

Katie and Blake had just arrived back from the village shop where they'd spent the last half hour buying up armfuls of salt 'n' vinegar crisps and Katie's favourite chocolate cream eggs.

Blake leaned back against a saddle rack looking decidedly yellow. Blake was staying with us until he found another job in a show-jumping yard, although I was keeping my fingers and toes crossed that he'd stay on at Hollywell. He was a brilliant rider and he was teaching me how to show-jump properly for the first time in my life.

"Of course, there's one thing we're all forgetting," Blake said as a serious afterthought, twiddling with Colorado's girth and looking pensive. "Sarah is going to hit the roof!"

Sarah was our stepmother and it had been her idea to set up the sanctuary after our dad died three years ago. She was like a big sister and she usually went along with all our plans but for some reason she had been dead against the letter to Rocky. We had never seen her so angry, she was normally so easy going. She had strictly forbidden Ross to send the letter but we had posted it anyway. None of us really believed anything would come of it and we couldn't see any harm in just sending it.

But Blake was right. She wasn't going to be very happy when she found out we had deliberately deceived her. In fact, she was going to be hopping mad. We had never gone behind her back before, but I still couldn't understand why she had got so upset.

*

4

"How could you do this to me?" she said, as we all sat in the kitchen looking guilty and feeling even worse.

Sarah had just arrived back from the printers who had proofed her latest manuscript and what she promised us was her best book yet. Sarah was a romantic novelist and she was seriously good, although it takes ages to get established as a well-known author.

Jigsaw, our golden retriever, had gone with her and now he was hysterically greeting us as if he hadn't seen us for years. As he slobbered all over Blake and bashed Sarah's prize Yucca plant with his tail Sarah clumped up and down the kitchen floor.

"Don't you see what he's doing?" she said, beating the teabags to a pulp in the teapot. "He's using us, it's the perfect publicity stunt. I can hear him now. Let's use Hollywell Stables to win a bit of good favour. Imagine the publicity, especially coming up to Christmas. It's the perfect PR stunt. It might even get him to number one for Christmas. Let's face it, his career needs a bit of a lift."

Sarah was boiling over with anger. I'd never seen her like this.

"You've never even met him," Ross blurted out, looking rebellious. "You've always told us not to judge someone before we've met them."

"That's not the point," Sarah said, whipping round from the kitchen sink, her long red hair flying into her face.

"Well, what is the point?" Ross answered back, getting more and more angry.

"You know very well," Sarah shouted, scaring Jigsaw who hid under the table. "We're not going to be some cheap gimmick for a clapped-out musician who's going nowhere. He ought to retire while he's still got some dignity. I'm sorry, but that's my last word on the matter. It's not on." And with that she stormed out of the kitchen to her office, slamming the door behind her so hard that it shook in its frame.

"Wow!" Katie said after a few minutes of silence. "Was that World War Three, or was that World War Three?"

I had never seen Sarah so angry, apart from when she had got stuck into a girl called Louella in the summer, but now she was being completely unreasonable. There had to be some explanation, something she wasn't telling us, and I, for one, was determined to find out what it was.

Chapter Two

As it turned out, Sarah didn't have much choice. The concert was going ahead and that was that – it was too late to pull out.

"I just don't understand her," Ross said, storming up and down, with his black hair falling into his eyes and his hands balling into tight fists of frustration. "It's just not fair. Doesn't she realize this is one of the best things that's ever happened to us?"

We all sat in the kitchen, cleaning tack and discussing the concert. Sarah was locked away in her office, busy working on her new novel.

"Will someone tell me what's happening?" Ross said, his eyes dark with anger.

"Ssssssh," I hissed, looking through the hall towards the study door.

"Because I'm telling you," Ross went on, "as sure as I'm standing here, I haven't got a clue."

He flopped down into an empty chair, raking his hair back in an exasperated gesture. "What is going on?"

And the trouble was, none of us knew. Sarah had just dropped her bombshell. While she couldn't do anything about the concert going ahead, she didn't want any of us to get involved. She had strictly forbidden us to go to the concert.

It was ridiculous. Outrageous. Ross had stormed out of the house in a fit of temper. Sarah had simply buried herself in her work.

"Look," Blake said, flinging Colorado's saddle on to the back of his chair, and looking as soured off as Ross, "what's the point of going on and on about it? There's nothing we can do, nothing. Not until we find out what's behind it all. So let's just drop it for five minutes, OK?"

Blake angled his gaze at Ross who was still seething with anger.

Ross grudgingly nodded his head, and then looked away. "OK," he said. "For now."

"Hallelujah!" Katie shrieked, and I agreed full force.

"Perhaps now we can get back to talking about Colorado?"

We were supposed to be discussing Colorado's trip to Olympia – to the Christmas horse show.

By some miracle, and partly Blake's genius, Colorado had qualified for a novice show-jumping class which was specially designed for newcomers. Blake had always said that Colorado would make a world-class show-jumper one day, but none of us ever expected him to be so good, so fast.

It was only a few months since Blake and I had rescued him. He used to be half crazy with fear, whereas now he had blossomed into a superb example of a show-jumper, rippling with steel-hard muscle and beautifully balanced in Blake's talented hands. We had spent the summer making practice jumps out of old tyres and barrels, anything we could get our hands on.

"We've got to see the Shetland Grand National," Katie stated emphatically as I read out the programme in every minute detail. She was sitting on the floor trying to groom Oswald and Matilda, our two black and white kittens, who were more interested in diving on my foot.

"And the police horses, and the pantomine!" Katie added, excitement whipping up inside her.

"I definitely want to see the dressage display," I said, marking it off with a bright red pen, and wondering how on earth we were going to fit it all in.

Blake started checking and re-checking his entry papers. There was so much to think about – overnight stabling, flu vaccinations, special competitor's badges, even the coach we had booked for us all to get down there. It would be terrible if anything went wrong. I didn't think I'd be able to sleep a wink until it was all over.

The shrill ring of the telephone cut into my thoughts.

"I'll get it," Ross volunteered, up to his eyes in saddle soap and quickly wiping his hands on the front of his jeans.

I took over oiling Colorado's show bridle while Blake kept saying over and over that he didn't think Colorado was ready.

Colorado was only 14.2 hands but he could out-jump any horse. He used to belong to our near neighbour, Louella, who was a junior show-jumper and had two 14.2 ponies called Royal Storm and the Wizard. Her uncle had sent Colorado over to England because he thought he was too good to be used as a cow horse, but Louella hated him from the very beginning. She thought his skewbald coat was too common looking and she despised his Mustang breeding.

From what we could gather from Louella's father, Mr Sullivan, Colorado had been a stallion roaming the plains of Colorado with his own herd of mares and foals. He had been caught by some cowhands who gelded him and then tried to break him in. Louella's father had bought him cheap because nobody could ride him.

Blake said it was Colorado's breeding which

made him so special. He had all the speed of his thoroughbred father and the sheer strength, stamina and spirit of his wild Mustang mother.

Because he had been left as a stallion until he was four years old he had developed a wonderfully well-crested and powerful neck. He truly was an impressive horse to look at and I never could understand why Louella hated him so much. But the truth was she was more frightened of him than anything else. He kept rearing up and in a fit of temper she had called in the vet to have him shot.

Blake and I had saved his life by kidnapping him in the middle of the night and hiding him at Hollywell. That was way back in the summer and a lot had happened since then. For one thing Louella's parents had split up and she had moved to America with her mother.

"What's happened?" I lurched in my seat, as Ross walked back into the kitchen from the hallway. He had just come off the phone and looked almost sea-sick.

"Guess who that was?" he said, turning pea green and leaning against the armchair. My stomach did a flip as I immediately imagined all our ponies running wild on the main road.

"Well, who was it?" I squawked, wanting to get any bad news over with.

"It was Rocky!" he said, "I've just been talking to a famous rock star!"

"You mean, he rang here personally?" Blake couldn't believe it.

"You bet he did," Ross said, getting back his composure and his colour. "And that's not the best of it . . . He's coming here tomorrow, he's coming to Hollywell Stables!"

None of us had expected this – not a personal visit. Now I knew for sure I wouldn't be able to sleep a wink.

The next morning was like a whirlwind. We were all working like fury to get the place spick and span. Ross was sweeping the yard so hard that the brush head flew off and hit Katie on the knee. I was bedding down stables and filling haynets as if there was no tomorrow. Blake was even polishing the stable windows with some special window cleaner pinched from under the kitchen sink.

We all felt as if we were about to explode with nervous energy.

"I wonder what he's like?" Katie mused for the hundredth time that morning.

"I bet he's all showbizzy and over-dramatic," Ross said, deliberately winding her up.

"Totally over the top," Blake added, finishing off the windows with a bit of old vest doubling as a duster. "And I bet he wears a wig and false teeth."

"Really?" Katie said, looking totally aghast and believing every word.

"I bet he's dead boring, and never laughs, not ever," I joined in the game.

"Oh, be serious," Katie said, looking about to pop with frustration. "It's not funny."

Preparations for the concert had been going ahead at the speed of light. Originally Rocky had planned to fit the gig into his schedule for next year, but now it was all go. They were going to squeeze it into Rocky's present tour, "The Return", and that meant just a week before Christmas! Rocky was making a big comeback after two years out of the limelight.

Nobody really knew what he had been doing over the past eighteen months but it was reported that his original manager had swindled him out of most of his fortune. It was rumoured that Rocky had sold his houses in Florida and Hollywood, even that he no longer owned his private jet and had nearly gone bankrupt. "The Return" was the first album he had released for three years and it was receiving rave reviews. Ross was saving up for the CD and I had already bought the single, *Miracle*, which was presently zooming up the charts.

It was reported on Radio One all day yesterday that his concert at Wembley stadium had been a knock-out success. Some of the tickets had been changing hands for over three hundred pounds and fans had been camping out in front of his hotel. No matter how hard I tried I couldn't imagine what it must feel like to be so famous. All I knew was that it must be incredibly glamorous.

Ross had once read in a newspaper article that Rocky came from Sheffield and he'd started out busking and then singing in pubs. His real name was Ronny Barraclough and in the early days he was known as "Rockin' Ronny". Now he was known to his millions of fans as simply Rocky and he was known the world over. It was an incredible story, especially as he had started out with just a second-hand guitar and he'd never had a singing lesson in his life. Unlike most rock stars, Rocky had a really good voice.

"This must be him!" Katie screeched like a half-crazed fanatic.

We all strained our ears as we heard a car engine but it was a false alarm. Sarah pulled into the drive just as Jigsaw knocked over a water bucket and sent it gushing into a pile of dirty straw.

Sarah had been to pick up Danny who was staying with us for Christmas. Danny was only just nine years old and he was very small for his age. His mother was always going off with her boyfriend and leaving him so Danny spent most of his holidays at Hollywell. He was like a member of the family and he and Katie were as thick as thieves.

It was Danny who had led us to a pony called Queenie who was lying close to death in a scrap-yard near to where Danny lived. She had belonged to two thugs called Bazz and Revhead who had left her tethered with no food, water or even shelter. When we found her she was suffocating from a piece of wire caught round her throat.

She was so thin it was heart-wrenching and it was touch and go for a long time as to whether she would survive. It was our little yearling Sophie who had given her the will to live. Queenie had become a sort of substitute mother and now she and Sophie were inseparable. Queenie was our lucky mascot and looking at her now it was hard to believe she was well over twenty years old and once the victim of neglect. If it wasn't for Danny's bravery in fetching help she wouldn't be here today. As soon as Queenie saw Danny she let out a great joyous whinny. Queenie loved all of us but Danny was special. Danny was her very best friend.

"He's here!" Katie yelled out like a blast from a fog horn. "It's him, he's here!" She and Jigsaw went racing off down the drive with Jigsaw barking like mad. I thought it was another false alarm until I caught sight of the white stretch limousine turning up our drive. My stomach did a somersault and I quickly flattened down my hair.

"Wow, look at this," Ross whispered in my ear as the limousine swished to a halt in the yard. The engine hardly made any noise at all and it was driven by a chauffeur wearing the full uniform, hat included.

Rocky was out in a flash before the chauffeur had a chance to open the door; and it was like someone turning on a mega-watt lightbulb. Katie was struck dumb and Danny's jaw had dropped to the floor.

Rocky was tall and ultra slim, dressed all in black and wearing a fantastic leather jacket – on the back was written in big gold letters, "Rocky – The Return".

But his most staggering feature was his hair. It was just like in his photographs only more impress-ive. It was very long – right down his back and jet black, but running all the way down the middle from his forehead to his hair ends was a huge white streak. It looked sensational.

"Well, don't just stand there gawping," Rocky said. "Introduce me!"

He was fantastic. Better than I'd ever dreamed. He was so friendly and down to earth and he wanted to see every horse and hear every rescue story. Even though he'd been living in America for a long time he still had some of his Yorkshire accent. He kept calling us luv and saying things like "blinkin' 'eck". Katie fell in love with him from the very minute he took her hand and she led him to Queenie's stable. Rocky adored Queenie and Danny plumped up his chest with pride although he hadn't managed to say a single word yet.

Rocky came inside for a cup of tea and Sarah brought out her best set of china. He had three sugars in his tea and devoured the chocolate biscuits as if he hadn't eaten for a week. Blake took a cup out to the limousine for the chauffeur, who refused to come inside. Ross asked Rocky loads of questions about his music and Sarah sat and listened and made no comment.

We'd always known that Rocky loved horses because it had been in loads of magazines about how he owned a racehorse and it was stabled in our area. It was for this reason that we had decided to write to Rocky rather than any other rock star. As Ross said, he obviously liked horses and he would be in our region at some time or other to see his horse. It all fitted.

What we didn't expect was what Rocky said next.

"Come with me!" he said, as if inviting us on a

mundane trip to the corner shop. "I'm just off to see Terence now."

Rocky had named his racehorse after his dad who had got him started in music and always believed in him. Even so, it was the funniest name for a racehorse that I'd ever heard.

Ross, Blake, Danny, Katie and myself piled into the big sleek limousine in some kind of trance. We were all shellshocked. Sarah had refused to come with us and insisted we go without her. At least she hadn't tried to stop us.

The inside of the limousine was like a palace. There were six seats in the back alone and a television set and a small table. There was a drinks cabinet and even a mini fridge. Blake and Ross were seriously impressed, especially when Rocky poured us all drinks of fresh orange juice and through the tinted windows we could see people staring at us.

Rocky was showing Danny how everything worked, from the electric windows to the air conditioning. Danny couldn't take his eyes off Rocky's hands. He had a ring on every finger, some were huge stones and they clinked together when he moved. It was all very glamorous. Danny still hadn't said a word since Rocky had arrived but his cheeks were flushed up pink and he was beaming from ear to ear.

"This must be it!" Katie shrieked, with her head half hanging out of the window.

Rocky had been telling us about his trainer, Tom Richards, who was one of the best trainers in the country, or at least he had been until last year when his wife died when the horse she was riding bolted into the path of a car. He hadn't had a winner since. Many of the owners had moved their horses elsewhere but Rocky didn't like to be disloyal.

When we arrived in the racing yard the trainer and the girl groom, or rather lass as they are called in racing, were waiting for us by one of the stables. Horses' heads were popping up everywhere; there must have been fifty to sixty boxes in all, although from what Rocky had said most of them must be empty.

Tom Richards shook Rocky's hand and introduced him to Hannah who was responsible for Terence. Mr Richards had wispy grey hair and watery eyes that kept running. He was small enough to be a jockey but he looked quite old – I noticed when he shook hands with Rocky that he was trembling quite badly.

Hannah went inside the stable and led out Terence. He was a beautiful bay thoroughbred with a dazzling coat that shone like a conker. Rocky said that he was a hurdler and he was entered for a

19

race in just four days' time! Hurdlers are horses that race over roughly two miles with small hurdles to jump instead of big fences.

Katie gave him a sliced carrot and he took it gently from her outstretched hand. He was clipped out and well rugged up which was a good job because the wind was biting. Rocky stroked his neck but didn't say much. Then he wandered off with Danny to look in some of the other boxes.

Hannah seemed nervous and kept looking down at her feet but I presumed it was because she was shy. Ross said he would do anything to own a horse like Terence, and Blake said he had near perfect conformation.

Back in the limousine we all piled into our seats, red faced from the fierce winds and ecstatic about Rocky's racehorse.

"We love him," I said, and really meant it. "He's one of the most beautiful horses I've ever seen."

Rocky looked preoccupied and not altogether with us.

"Thanks, luv," he said quickly, stroking back his long hair which had blown all over the place. "But there's just one slight problem," he added.

"What's that?" Ross asked, leaning over to help Danny turn up the heating.

"*That's not my horse!*"

Chapter Three

"What do you mean?" we all shrieked like banshees, but Rocky refused to say another word until we were back in the warmth of Hollywell and drinking hot Bovril.

"How can you be sure?"

"I just know, that's all, I just know that's not Terence."

"But you haven't seen him for six months," Ross protested. "And before that only a couple of times from what I can gather."

Rocky was sitting in the armchair with no springs, nursing Matilda who was kneading his lap with her tiny claws. Oswald was in the corner looking sulky.

"I just know," Rocky said. "Besides," he added, looking thoughtful, "when I first bought him I noticed that he had a funny whorl of hair on his neck under his mane – when I looked on that horse there was nothing."

"But he was clipped out," Ross said logically.

Most horses had funny whorls of hair, either

on their forehead, neck or chest and they were called rosettes.

"You'd still be able to tell though," Rocky said. "Even though the hair is shaved short."

"He's right," Blake said, "but you'd have to look closely."

"So if that's not Terence," Ross said, scooping up little Oswald, "who on earth is it?"

"A ringer," Sarah spoke up, standing by the sink and yanking off her bright yellow rubber gloves.

It was the first time she'd said anything since we sat down to discuss it.

A dawning light washed over Blake's face. "But he wouldn't, surely, he wouldn't dare . . . would he?"

"What's a ringer?" Katie piped up, just as I was about to ask the same thing.

"A ringer," Sarah explained, "is when the trainer swops one horse for another identical one, usually less good. It's illegal and it's done so they can fix the race and make more money on the betting."

Katie looked confused and Sarah explained it all again. Ross said he'd read all about it in a Dick Francis book.

"Chances are," Sarah said, "he's already sold Terence, which is risky, or he's still got him and he's waiting to swop them back when it suits him."

Rocky looked horrified. "But I've always trusted

Tom," he said, unable to believe that his trainer could double-cross him.

"From what you say about his finances," Blake said, "he could be a desperate man."

I remembered what Rocky had said about the racing stables being half empty.

"The question is," Sarah said, "do we go to the police?"

"No," Rocky said, leaping up without thinking and sending Matilda flying. "Ross is right, I could be wrong, and besides the press would have a field day."

"OK, OK, no police," Ross said. "But *what* then?"

"I've got an idea," Katie piped up, perched in front of the Christmas tree with Danny and Jigsaw.

"Oh, yeah, like what? We dress up as cowboys and do a raid on the place?" Ross joked.

Katie pulled a face and told him to shut up. Sarah told them both to act their age.

"Let's hear it," Rocky said unexpectedly, looking straight at Katie and waiting for her suggestion.

Ross looked put out and I couldn't help but smirk.

"It's simple," Katie said. "We wait till it's dark and then we go to the racing yard."

"What for?" I said, looking blank.

"To find Terence, of course," Katie answered, looking at me as if I was dim.

"But that's trespassing," I added.

"Since when has that ever stopped us?" Ross joined in, putting a bauble back on the Christmas tree which Jigsaw had just sent flying.

The last time we went snooping, Ross had got into a fight with Revhead and ended up breaking an arm.

"It's dangerous," Sarah said, looking grave.

"But there's no alternative," Rocky added, weighing up the pros and cons. "How else am I ever going to know what's going on?"

"Let's put it to the vote," I suggested, trying to be the voice of reason.

"All those in favour raise their hands!" Rocky shouted.

We all stuck our hands in the air apart from Sarah, who thought we were all mad. Danny tried to lift Jigsaw's paw but Rocky said that didn't count.

"Let's do it!" Danny yelled, getting over-excited and then suddenly feeling shy.

Sarah shrugged her shoulders and Katie handed out Christmas crackers by way of a celebration. As mine went off with a loud bang I wondered what on earth we were getting ourselves into. Ross stuck a paper hat on my head and I deliberately

24

pushed all feelings of doubt to the back of my mind. After all, it was our job to save horses. And if the real Terence was in trouble it was up to us to find him, whatever the consequences.

"How do I look?" Sarah asked the next morning, parading round the kitchen in high heels and an expensive tweed suit.

She had reluctantly agreed to our plan to find Terence but first she'd insisted on visiting the stables herself. She said Tom Richards wouldn't know her and she could pretend to be a prospective racehorse owner. She could look in all the stables when Mr Richards gave her a guided tour and hopefully she'd spot a Terence lookalike.

Rocky thought it was a good idea and so did Ross and Blake. Rocky even suggested paying for a taxi to conjure up the right image. Our old Volvo was so battered it wasn't the kind of car a potential racehorse owner would arrive in. Sarah had agreed and now the taxi was pipping its horn outside on the drive.

"Good luck!" we all shouted.

"And take care," Ross yelled, but I don't think Sarah heard him.

Rocky had to fly off to do a television interview and we had five stables to muck out.

"Do you think it will work?" Katie asked, pushing our squeaky wheelbarrow into Queenie's empty stable and knocking over the pitchfork in the process. We had turned the horses out in the field in their all-weather rugs which kept them warm. Katie was wearing so many clothes she looked like an Eskimo and she still complained of the cold.

"I don't know," I answered, thinking of Sarah trying to be a super sleuth and telling Mr Richards a pack of lies.

But we needed proof more than anything else. At the moment all we had was Rocky's word that something dodgy was going on. What if Rocky was wrong?

Sarah had surprised us all last night when in a moment of weakness she had agreed that we could go to the concert. Ross had been struck speechless and Katie had said that Rocky was a forty carat dude whatever that meant. Blake said Katie watched too many old Western movies.

Sarah was still not happy about the concert but Rocky had assured her there would be no publicity. Surely though in order to get donations for Hollywell, publicity was exactly what we did need? It didn't make sense. I also had an uneasy feeling that Rocky might not be all that he seemed. Surely he was just too nice to be believable?

"Mel, are you listening to me?" Ross was tugging the pitchfork out of my hand and yelling something in my earhole.

"Come on, it's Blake!" he yelled. "He's had an accident."

My heart almost stopped dead. "Blake? How? Where?"

Ross dragged me towards the field where Blake had been schooling Colorado over some new jumps, but I couldn't see him anywhere.

"Blake?" I yelled, panic setting in with a deathly grip.

"He's all right," Ross said. "He's not hurt."

"Well, thanks for telling me!" I screamed, furious that he'd allowed me to think the worst.

"What happened?" I yelled, ploughing through the mud towards Blake and Colorado who were stood sheltering under a tree and looking thoroughly miserable. Colorado's head was hanging between his knees and Blake was trying to lift up his near foreleg.

"It's nothing," Blake said, looking far from all right, splattered with mud and grass stains, and blood trickling from the corner of his mouth where he said he'd cut his lip.

"Mel, don't panic, he's OK," Blake insisted as I ran my hand down Colorado's legs. It would be terrible if anything happened to him this close to Olympia.

"He's just grazed his knee," Blake said. "And he's a bit shaken up, that's all."

We led them back to the stables while Blake explained what had happened. Apparently Ross had been putting up a jump for Blake – just the usual kind of spread – and Colorado had freaked out on the approach, somehow landing in the middle of it. Poles lay strewn all over and the ground was cut to ribbons.

"You didn't see it, Mel," Ross said. "Colorado rolled right on top of him."

As Blake handed me Colorado's reins he leaned on Ross's arm for support. "What's wrong with your leg?"

Blake had sprained his ankle. Or at least that was what it looked like to me but I was no expert.

"Where's that bandage?" Ross shouted to Katie who was rummaging around in the horses' medical cabinet.

"I'm all right," Blake insisted, with his leg propped up on a chair.

Katie came back from the medicine cabinet with a veterinary bandage, antiseptic ointment and an Animalintex poultice. "Will this do?"

"Of course, nobody's considered what this means," I said, slapping some ice cubes on the swelling and causing Blake to wince. "Sprained ankles don't go away overnight."

"We'll have to cut down your riding boot," Ross said. "I've seen some of the top riders do that."

"I don't care if I break every bone in my body," Blake grimaced. "I'm riding at Olympia."

It was my dream one day to be a famous show-jumper and I knew that if I were Blake I would feel exactly the same way.

What I couldn't understand was why Colorado had gone so crazy at that jump. They were new poles we had borrowed from the Pony Club, but even so, he'd never refused a jump in his life, let alone smashed into one.

"What if he's lost his nerve?" Blake said, sounding worried sick.

It was very possible. Some horses did lose their nerve after a fall, and so did the riders. It was even worse if they couldn't get back on straight away and clear another jump.

"Don't talk like that," I said, trying to sound positive but feeling a bundle of nerves inside. "It will be OK." But a little voice whispered in my head that trouble always came in threes and there was definitely more to come.

"Well, that was a complete and utter waste of time," Sarah said, flouncing down into an armchair and nearly crushing Katie's special horsey advent calendar. "That man was impossible."

"I presume you didn't find Terence?" Blake asked, sprawled straight out on the settee with three bandages wrapped round his ankle and a wet dishcloth on his forehead.

"Didn't get the chance to look," Sarah frothed, her red hair falling loose and making her look slightly demented. "That man was enough to drive anyone to madness. All he wanted to talk about was money."

Sarah was talking about Rocky's trainer, Mr Richards. The trip to the racing stables had been a disaster. We still didn't have a clue what had happened to the real Terence.

Sarah came back from the fridge clutching a packet of jam doughnuts and accidentally knocking Blake's ankle which caused him to screech in pain.

"There was one thing though," Sarah said, munching into a doughnut and oozing jam on to the carpet. She always got hungry when she was upset.

"That Hannah, the groom who looks after Terence . . ."

I thought back to the girl who had led the bay thoroughbred out of the stable. She had been shy and uneasy but I hadn't thought anything of it at the time.

"Yes?" we all said eagerly, gripping the edges of our seats.

"She knows something," Sarah said. "There's definitely something she's not telling us."

"Well, it's now or never." Rocky's voice came from the front seat of our old Volvo as the darkness closed in.

We were parked in a lay-by a quarter of a mile from the racing stables and I was seriously wondering whether my nerves could stand the strain. I was in the back by myself and Ross was in the front next to Rocky. It was well past midnight and the wind was blasting through the trees.

Katie was furious that she had to stay behind but Sarah had insisted it was too dangerous, and Blake couldn't walk across the kitchen let alone do a midnight trek.

"Have you both got your torches?" Rocky asked, peering into the back where I sat quivering like a nervous wreck, my heart doing somersaults and my stomach twisting into tight knots.

We had decided to take our car because the limousine was too noticeable and might be recognized. Rocky had insisted on parking well up the road and out of sight.

"OK, let's do it," Rocky said, taking the initiative as we set off into the night like a bunch of escaped convicts.

"Over here," Rocky hissed as we sidled along a brick wall towards yet another row of stables.

I could hear horses shuffling and munching at their haynets but it was pitch black and I couldn't see a thing.

"Watch out," Ross whispered as I nearly cracked my leg on something hard which turned out to be a fire extinguisher.

It was freezing cold and pouring down with rain and up to now we hadn't seen anything which even resembled Terence.

"In here," Rocky mouthed, sliding the bolt back on a stable door ever so gently.

"Is it Terence?" I whispered, my jaw practically frozen up from the cold.

Rocky shone his torch into the box and picked out a bay horse standing asleep with its back to us.

"Is it him?" I hissed, praying it was the real Terence so we could get back to the car before we got caught.

The horse snorted and wheeled round as we all pressed into the stable to take a better look. But as it turned to face us, disappointment dragged at our hearts: it had a white star on its forehead. It wasn't Terence.

"What was that?" Rocky said as we all stood

stock still and practically stopped breathing.

"What?" Ross whispered behind me as we inched back into the woodshavings to stay out of sight.

Seconds passed which seemed to last like hours.

Then I heard it ... footsteps. On the gravel outside.

A cold finger of fear crept up my back and I felt like screaming.

There it was again. More footsteps. Pause. A flashlight.

Suddenly the steps moved quickly, purposefully towards us. The light flashed raw and bright into the stable and hurt my eyes, causing me to blink rapidly and ruining my night vision.

A pale face peered over the door with rat tails of wet hair dripping into her eyes.

It was Hannah.

We were so shocked we just stood there gaping.

"How did you know we were here?" Rocky said at last.

"Listen, there's no time to explain," Hannah said, looking more scared than any of us. "I need your help." Her eyes blurred with easy tears and openly pleaded with us.

"I'm desperate," she said. "It's Dancer. I think she's got pneumonia."

Chapter Four

"Who's Dancer?" Ross asked as we raced back to the car with Hannah who was obviously very distraught.

"You've got to tell us everything," Ross said, as we finally made it to the car.

"I will, I will," she said impatiently. "Just as soon as we get there."

The road loomed up dark and ominous ahead of us.

"Down here!" Hannah screeched, winding down the steamed-up window so she could get a better view.

Rocky slammed on the brakes and we all jerked forward.

"Quick, she's down here," she yelled, almost fighting to get out of the door before Rocky had even stopped the car.

The lane we had turned down was so rutted it was like driving over craters. The car felt as if it was going to fall to pieces at any minute.

"Here!" Hannah yelled. "Stop the car!"

We had pulled up in front of a farm gate in the middle of nowhere. I was still reeling from the shock of everything happening so fast. We had set out to find Terence and ended up chasing after a sick horse called Dancer.

Apparently Dancer was a horse that Hannah used to look after at the racing stables before Terence arrived. Dancer had disappeared a few months back and the trainer Tom Richards had refused to tell her where.

"Over here!" Rocky yelled, flashing the torchlight along a hedgerow. We had all climbed over the gate and were scouring the field shouting "Dancer". The wind was howling non-stop and my ears were freezing.

We still hadn't found her. An owl tooted somewhere above and made me jump out of my skin. Hannah was going crazy running up and down shouting her head off.

"I've found her!" Ross yelled, picking up the outline of a horse in the light of his torch. I blundered forward in the dark because my batteries had just gone kaput.

She was standing in a hollow with her back to the driving rain. Her head was slung low and she hardly noticed as we all moved towards her.

"Oh my God," Rocky muttered, raising his hand to her neck and then looking away.

She was in a desperate state. In fact, I had never seen a horse look so bad. It was probably worse because she was drenched through, which showed up every bone and poverty mark. Her eyes were totally glazed over and stuck out from her head which seemed huge in proportion to her body. Her mane and tail were matted and uncared for and her narrow body was shivering uncontrollably. Every so often her sides would heave in great spasms and there was thick mucus running out of both nostrils.

"It looks bad," Ross said, and I wasn't sure whether the wet on his face was from the rain or his eyes.

"You poor girl," I kept mumbling over and over as I rubbed at her ears in a feeble attempt to warm her up. I didn't know what else to do.

"We'd better get James," Ross said, looking out over the fields with his back to Dancer. He was talking about our vet, who had helped save Queenie's life and who was always there when we needed him.

"And the RSPCA, and we'd better get some transport," I added, thinking practically when all the time my heart was screaming out with rage that anybody could do this to a horse.

"We're taking you back to Hollywell," I whis-

pered to Dancer, and prayed that we weren't too
late.

"It's bad," James said in a solemn voice as he came
out of the stable, having examined Dancer.

We had put her in our special isolation unit at
the bottom of our five acre field. It had once been
an old cowshed which Blake and I had used to hide
Colorado when we first brought him to Hollywell.
Since then we had made it into a proper stable just
in case we ever had an infectious horse.

"I'm not going to lie to you," James said, rubbing at his temples with his fingers and looking
about to drop. He had been on emergencies all
night and it was now three o'clock in the morning.

"Hannah was right. She's got pneumonia."

We had always agreed that when it came to
running a sanctuary we had to prepare ourselves
for death and the fact that we couldn't save every
horse or pony that was brought to us. But when
James told us the bad news it hurt more than I
thought possible.

Hannah burst into tears and Sarah put her arm
round her shoulder. Ross offered her a straw bale
to sit on and then said he'd go and make a flask
of sweet tea.

Blake came out of Dancer's stable with his head

bowed low and clutching James' stethoscope.

"I'll sit with her!" I suddenly announced, determined to do this no matter what the others said.

James had explained to us that Dancer would need round the clock nursing. It was vital that she had all the love and care it was humanly possible to give, and I knew that alone might mean the difference between life and death.

"Mel's got a point," Sarah said, when I explained my reasons.

Blake was due at Olympia in a few days and it was of paramount importance that Colorado didn't catch the disease. Whoever nursed Dancer would not be able to go near the other horses. Sarah was working to a deadline with her new novel and she was already well behind. Katie and Danny were too young which just left me and Ross, and eventually we both agreed to take it in turns.

"Pneumonia in horses is very rare," James told us. "To be honest, it's the first case I've seen. It's usually caused from a primary viral infection and this is what's happened to Dancer. She's got so weak and run down from the infection that pneumonia's set in."

"The game's not over until the fat lady sings," Rocky said, which Sarah roughly translated to mean it wasn't over yet.

"What we need is a miracle," I added, and sincerely wished for some kind of hot-line to heaven.

"Despite how bad it looks," James said, "I think she'll pull through, I've injected her with antibiotics and I'm hoping that will bring her round."

"Look at the time," Hannah suddenly shrieked, holding a torch to the face of her watch. "I've got to get back, I'll lose my job."

Hannah had insisted from the start that she remain anonymous in this whole business. If Mr Richards found out that she was behind the rescue, he'd fire her on the spot. Jobs in racing were hard to come by and Hannah desperately wanted to be a jockey.

"I'll drive you back," Rocky said, looking completely exhausted with his hair stuck up on end and his leather jacket mud-splattered and ripped.

"If you want to see Terence again," Hannah said, catching hold of his arm, "you'll stay out of this."

"What?" Rocky said, taken aback.

"I mean it," she warned, looking at us with deadly serious eyes. "Don't let them know Rocky was involved in Dancer's rescue."

I sat down in a corner of Dancer's stable with Hannah's words weighing heavily on my heart.

What did she mean by *them*? Who was she talking about?

But I had other things on my mind, like nursing Dancer. As soon as she had come into the stable with the thick straw banked up round the sides she had laid down. Her eyelids kept flickering every now and then as if she was just checking that I was still there. Her breathing came in wheezes and sounded thick and heavy in her lungs.

I wrapped an extra horse blanket round my legs and sat there feeling numb all over and listening to the darkness outside. I had never sat up all night with a horse before and it was a bit scary, especially as it was in the middle of a field with nothing in sight. Ross had set up an old deck chair for me to sit in and I had the light turned on and a book to read but I couldn't concentrate. How could I when Dancer was so ill?

"You all right?" Sarah's voice in the doorway terrified me half to death. Dawn was just breaking and she had brought me another flask of hot soup. I didn't think I'd ever be able to look at tomato soup again without thinking of Dancer.

"How is she?" Sarah asked, trying not to make a noise so as not to disturb her.

Dancer hadn't lifted her head up all night but at least she'd had a good rest. In the light of the stable her delicate grey coat stood out and she didn't look half so dark now her coat had dried. She had a soft, rose pink nose and gentle eyes but they looked vacant and defeated.

"She's OK," I said to Sarah, "She's going to be fine."

Sarah then filled me in on what Hannah had quickly told her while James had been examining Dancer.

I couldn't believe it.

Dancer had been in training at the racing yard but she hadn't lived up to expectations. Everybody thought she had the potential to win a Classic, probably the Oaks, but then for no reason at all she suddenly stopped wanting to race. She refused to go out on the gallops and kept running backwards and rearing up. When she threw the yard's star jockey, Colin Jensen, nobody wanted to ride her and she was left in her stable.

Her owner pulled a dirty trick when he ran off to Spain leaving all his debts behind him and deserting poor Dancer. Mr Richards was furious and vowed to shoot her. Hannah said this was just an excuse since his wife had been killed on a grey horse and he thought Dancer was a bad omen.

The next bit really sent me goggle-eyed. Apparently Dancer was from one of the best blood-lines in the world, the Crimson Dancer line. Crimson Dancer only happened to be her grandfather!

It was bizarre. I'd read about legendary race-horses but to think that this poor neglected horse in front of me was related to them!

"Hannah said he decided to breed from her," Sarah explained, meaning Mr Richards and spitting the words out with venom. "That's why he chucked her out in a field rather than getting rid of her. He thought he could make some money from her foal."

"Poor Hannah," I said, thinking how awful it must be to care for a horse and then for it just to disappear and not know what's happened to it. "I wonder why he didn't tell her?" I said. "And how did she find out where Dancer was?"

But Sarah had something else to tell me and it wasn't good.

"I've just heard on the early breakfast news," she said, standing up to stretch her legs. "Rocky's hotel was broken into last night."

She paused briefly, unsure how to word her next phrase.

"Rocky has disappeared."

Chapter Five

Rocky was missing. Nobody knew where he was.

But that was the last thing on my mind right now. Dancer had deteriorated. She was going downhill fast and there was nothing I could do.

"You've got to save her," I whispered to James who was reading a thermometer and looking as if all was lost. "Please, James, do something."

Dancer was panting like a dog, her eyes half closed and glazed over. She was lying down in the straw with her legs and head stretched out limp and lifeless and her rib cage rising and falling as she panted. Dark patches of sweat broke out on her neck yet, when I touched her, she was cold and clammy.

It is very unusual for horses to lie down when they are surrounded by strange people, so I knew that Dancer must be seriously ill.

"Her temperature's rocketed," James said, wiping the thermometer clean with some cotton wool. "It's a hundred-and-five!"

The normal temperature for a horse was

100–101°F, which meant that Dancer was burning up.

"She's extremely weak," James said, looking in Dancer's eyes and then taking her pulse. "I've no option, I'm going to have to put her on a drip."

I never even knew that horses could be put on a drip.

"It's the best thing for her," James went on. "It usually works pretty fast."

"Let's try anything," Sarah said from the doorway where she was standing with Ross and Blake.

For one fleeting moment Dancer lifted her neck off the straw and then flopped down again.

"We'd better hurry," James said.

I stayed with Dancer while Ross went back to the car with James. They seemed to be gone for ages and all the time Dancer's breathing was getting faster. She had turned from cold and clammy to boiling hot and her head felt as if it was on fire.

"Mel, I really don't think you ought to watch this," James said when he came back into the stable with all the equipment.

But there was no way I was going to leave Dancer now. It was our job to save horses and ponies no matter what we had to go through ourselves.

"It looks worse than it actually is," James said as he pulled out a massive drip bag that was attached to some coiled plastic. "I'm basically going to pump in five litres of saline solution straight into her jugular vein. We can attach the bag to that beam up there." James pointed at the roof. Five litres seemed an enormous amount, but James assured us it would be all right.

He then got out a blunt-ended needle which he said was called a cannula. It was the biggest needle I'd ever seen. It was all of three-and-a-half inches long and nearly as thick as a pen. I had to swallow hard when James said he was going to stick the whole lot in the front of Dancer's neck. Surely it couldn't be done?

"First of all, I'll get the drip set up," James said. "I'm going to pump more antibiotics into her bloodstream and Finadyne, which is a bit like a glorified aspirin. It's vital that I get the drip attached to the needle as soon as it's in place. We don't want any blood clots."

Ross offered to hold the drip and James set to work.

"It's all right, girl," I said to Dancer, who lay resting, unaware of what was about to happen.

As soon as James was ready with the needle, he moved round to the front of Dancer's neck. My stomach was swirling. Even Sarah had turned a funny shade of green.

I gently cradled Dancer's head in my lap, all the

while stroking her, comforting her, telling her she was a brave girl.

"Hold her still, Mel," James said, running his hand up and down her neck to find the main artery, his face puckered up with concentration. "OK, here goes."

The needle went in easier than I'd expected. It was all over within seconds. Dancer jolted her head up, knocking me off balance and nearly catching James with one of her front legs which lashed out at empty air. James worked fast to attach the drip as blood swushed out from the cannula into the plastic coil. Sarah winced and I had to look the other way.

"Brave little girl," James patted Dancer's head. "It's all over now."

Dancer settled back down with the cannula in place and the drip suspended above her. James had secured the plastic coil up round the top of her head to stop her getting caught up in it and the needle coming out.

"Come on, girl, hang in there," I whispered into Dancer's ear, trying to will her to live.

"What are her chances?" Sarah asked, trying not to look at the drip.

"It depends," James answered, collecting up his things as quietly as he could. "We'll know more in the next hour. All we can do in the meantime is wait."

The next hour seemed like the longest in my whole life. Sarah made mugs of tea and handed out sausage rolls and I kept my fingers and toes crossed and prayed for a miracle.

We didn't tell Katie and Danny what was happening, so they sat in the house making a cardboard house for Oswald and Matilda, complete with beds, curtains and windows. Katie kept crowing that we now had six horses at the sanctuary and none of us had the heart to tell her that Dancer might not survive.

Outside, the drip was gradually going down, oozing its way into Dancer's bloodstream.

"Not long now," James said, when it was nearly half empty, and I wondered what he thought was going to happen.

I soon found out.

"Quick!" Ross yelled. "She's getting up!"

James flew across to the stable shouting instructions to Ross. I ran after him, throwing down my sausage roll, half-eaten. Dancer was staggering around the stable like a drunkard, swaying on her legs and shaking her head. James grabbed hold of the plastic coil in the nick of time before it dislodged the needle.

"She's up!" I yelled to Sarah who was running

after me with one welly on and another half off.

"I don't believe it," I cried, patting Dancer's head like mad.

"I knew there was a chance," James said. "But I didn't want to get everyone's hopes up."

Sarah gave James a big bear hug and I swallowed back tears of relief. Ross started singing the words to Rocky's hit single, *Miracle*. "Dreams can come true, never give in." It didn't sound anywhere near as good as when Rocky sung it, but who cared? Blake was just telling me that my face was so red it looked like an inflated strawberry when a familiar voice boomed out from directly behind me.

"What's going on then?"

We all turned round.

"Well, don't just stand there gawping," Rocky said, as large as life in the open doorway. "What's going on?"

James insisted that we all wash our hands and arms before we even went near any of the other animals. We left Dancer wrapped up in horse blankets and resting peacefully, and Rocky brought a bottle of champagne in from the limousine to celebrate.

"Of course she's got a long way to go yet,"

James said, but deep down I knew that Dancer was over the worst.

Jigsaw went hysterical with excitement when he saw Rocky and leapt straight at him, completely missed and went flying into the Christmas tree for the second time in two days.

"Oh, no," Sarah groaned as the Christmas fairy shot into the air and landed splat in the middle of the flower display.

Danny sneezed when the bubbles of the champagne went straight up his nose and Rocky proposed a toast to Dancer and her good health.

"But what we all want to know," I said to Rocky and speaking for all of us, "is what happened to you?"

"Oh, that was nothing," Rocky said, passing it off with a sweep of his hand. "I just had to do a runner, that's all."

"So there was no great mystery?" Sarah said. And then Rocky explained how the press had blown it all out of proportion.

Some of his fans had broken into the hotel, about twenty or thirty. They were trying to find Rocky's suite of rooms but had ended up bursting into a dentist's convention. Rocky had escaped out of a fire exit and booked into another hotel but nobody knew that at the time. Katie wasn't the only one to think he'd been kidnapped.

"So, here I am," Rocky said, looking pale as paper with dark smudges of exhaustion under both eyes. We were all the worst for wear after a sleepless night. Also "The Return" tour had taken a lot out of Rocky but he was too stubborn to admit it.

"So how about staying on here?" Sarah said, out of the blue and knocking me for six.

The concert was only the day after next and Rocky's fans were sure to invade his new hotel in the meantime. It made perfect sense.

"Yippee!" yelled Katie who had been secretly guzzling at Sarah's champagne.

"You mean stay at Hollywell?" Rocky said, looking shell-shocked.

"Well, why not?" Sarah said. All her reservations about Rocky seeming to have disappeared.

"It would be a privilege," Rocky said, winking at me and raising his glass. "Here's to Hollywell Stables."

Rocky went back to his hotel to pick up his gear while Sarah was glued to the phone all afternoon talking to the RSPCA Inspector and dealing with Tom Richards who was cursing us from here to Timbuktoo. You could hear his voice from right across the room and Sarah said later that she thought he'd been drinking because he was slurring his words.

Katie surprised everyone by deciding to take Jigsaw for a walk, but really it was an excuse to visit the village hall. Rocky's people were doing all the organizing for the concert which meant we didn't have to lift a finger. Hopefully the money raised would be enough for us to buy a horse trailer, which we desperately needed. Then, of course, we'd have to convert it into a special horse ambulance with a mechanical lifting ramp and winching equipment which would all cost extra money. Often when horses were badly treated they were just too weak to walk and literally had to be lifted into the horsebox.

Sarah insisted that I go with Katie and Danny and Jigsaw to keep a sisterly eye on matters and just in case they proved a nuisance.

When we arrived at the hall there were masses of Rocky's people rigging up lighting and a stage area. They wouldn't let anyone inside and they all rushed around looking terribly important and very busy. The men all had designer stubble and wore leather jackets and the women stomped around shouting at everybody and marking things off on their clipboards.

Katie and I managed to get inside for a look only because we were wearing our special red Hollywell

Stables sweatshirts. The lighting director had been so impressed he'd ordered two for his kids and even decided on a turquoise green one for himself. We also had special Hollywell Christmas cards with a photograph of Queenie on the front and he agreed to buy a box of those too, which was wonderful – he hadn't even seen them!

When we got back to Hollywell, there was a strange car parked in the driveway: a pale blue Mercedes which I instantly recognized as belonging to Mr Sullivan. What did *he* want?

Mr Sullivan was Louella's father. He had given Colorado to the sanctuary in the summer rather than have him shot or sold at a sale to the meat man. We had it in writing that Colorado belonged to Hollywell Stables and Mr Sullivan would pay his upkeep for at least the next year. It was a kind of guilt money after his daughter Louella's cruelty to Colorado. So why had he turned up out of the blue? And where was everybody? The yard was deserted. Queenie, Sophie and Bluey were standing cold and anxious at the field gate waiting to be brought in and the teatime feeds hadn't even been made up. Colorado was banging at his stable door as if he hadn't been fed for a week.

Suddenly Blake came out of the house with Mr

Sullivan, his face anxious and strained. I had a terrible feeling something awful had happened.

"Is it bad?" I asked Blake as soon as Mr Sullivan had gone.

Blake was so spaced out he could hardly speak. "Bad?" he repeated. "Mel – it's only absolutely, completely, unbelievably brilliant!

"Of course it all depends on how well I do," Blake went on, his eyes sparkling with enthusiasm.

Ross came back from checking on Dancer to say that she'd started eating her bran mash and she'd had a good drink of water. Blake couldn't contain himself any longer and blurted out the whole story.

Mr Sullivan had promised that if Blake won or got placed at Olympia, he would sponsor him and also give him rides on Louella's other horses, the Wizard and Royal Storm. Mr Sullivan was going to set him up in his own show-jumping yard! It was fantastic, just the opportunity Blake needed.

"Talk about pressure though," Blake said. "What if I lose?"

"You won't," I said, "you're both brilliant."

"Not the other day we weren't when we crashed into that fence," Blake said, remembering his accident.

"What about your ankle?" Ross asked, full of concern.

It was still blown up like a balloon and Sarah was convinced he'd chipped the bone.

"Stuff that!" Blake said. "There's no way I'm going to let a stupid ankle hold me back ... But there is one problem," Blake added, his face darkening. "I'm convinced Colorado screwed up at that fence for a reason. So I tried out a little experiment with Sarah's yellow rubber gloves. It's the colour," Blake said. "Colorado's scared of yellow. That's what was wrong with that jump – it was yellow."

Blake explained how nobody really knows if horses can see in colour, but experiments have proven that it is easier for a horse to see yellow and green than blue and red. Blake said he knew of a horse who was terrified of yellow because his owner had attacked him with a lunge whip while wearing a yellow coat.

This was the last thing we needed. Blake was leaving for Olympia tomorrow morning. There was no time to get Colorado right.

"Well, we'll just have to pray there's no yellow jump in the competition," Ross said.

"Anyone got a Bible?" Blake said. "I think I'm going to need a miracle, never mind about Lady Luck."

I spent the last hour of daylight helping Blake clip Colorado. He'd already been clipped at the beginning of the winter, so he just needed tidying up. Blake had groomed him until his coat was gleaming all over. His white patches were dazzling and Blake had washed his brown and white tail in a special rinse which had made it shine more than ever. He'd even rubbed in a touch of olive oil to make it look extra glossy. Colorado had never looked more beautiful. He was like something out of a fairy story.

"Who's this?" Blake said, looking up as the familiar white limousine zoomed up the drive. Someone got out wearing dark glasses and a blonde wig which had tipped slightly to one side.

"What do you think?" Rocky shouted, pointing to his new disguise.

"Well, it didn't fool us," Blake laughed, and I couldn't stop giggling when Jigsaw kept trying to jump up and pull it off.

"Where on earth did you dig that up from?" Ross asked, examining Rocky's wig which he said looked more like a stuffed hamster.

"Never you mind," Rocky said, plonking it back on his head, and fixing it in front of the mirror.

"This is to keep the fans at bay. If I'm going to stay here, I don't want you getting over-run. It's all got to be top secret . . . Do you know I walked into the village shop and got mugged by three old ladies in head scarves? They thought I was Cliff Richard, I mean, do I look like Cliff Richard?"

There was only one answer to that – definitely not!

James and Sarah had gone off Christmas shopping. It was James's only day off and Sarah had dragged him out kicking and squealing with a list of things to buy. James and Sarah had been seeing each other romantically for the past six months, but insisted they were just good friends. Of course we knew better. James always got embarassed when Katie hummed "Here Comes the Bride" and Sarah had even invited James for Christmas dinner. Everybody could see they were mad about each other which was just fine with us because James was terrific.

"I've found out all about Terence," Rocky said, out of the blue and taking us all by surprise.

"What?" Ross said.

And then Rocky told us how he'd been to the racing stables that afternoon and Tom Richards had suspected nothing about his involvement in the rescue of Dancer.

"Boy! Was he in a bad mood though," Rocky said, devouring a packet of chocolate biscuits and swilling away a half pint mug of tea with a picture of a mare and foal on the front.

Apparently Hannah had taken Rocky to one side at the stables while Tom Richards went back to his office to fetch Rocky's bill. She was desperate to find out more about Dancer but she also had news of Terence, or at least the horse that was standing in for Terence.

"Now let me get this right," I said, trying to make sense of what Rocky was telling us.

"Your racehorse, the real Terence, is missing, and Mr Richards has put his own bay thoroughbred lookalike in Terence's place."

"That's right," Rocky said, reaching for another chocolate biscuit and giving half to Jigsaw who was slobbering all over the place. "That was the horse we saw at the yard."

"OK, so where is your horse?" I asked, trying to keep up with Rocky's explanation.

"If I knew that I wouldn't be sitting here," Rocky spluttered, spraying biscuit crumbs across the table. "But this is what I've found out from Hannah," he said, and went on to tell us the full story.

It turned out that Rocky's real horse had suffered a sort of equine nervous breakdown. Often in racing if a horse isn't doing very well they'll just leave it in the stable and hardly bother to exercise it. I'd heard the occasional story of horses coming out of training yards hardly being able to walk because they'd been shut up so much.

Poor Terence had been just such a horse. Mr Richards was short staffed as it was. Hannah said they were working all hours, often not finishing till late at night and then starting at six in the morning. Mr Richards' attitude was that he'd seen these famous people before. They buy a horse on a whim and then forget about it so why shouldn't he?

As a result Terence had become dangerous with frustration and neglect. When Rocky rang up to say that he wanted to see his horse Mr Richards had panicked. He couldn't let Rocky see Terence in the state he was in so he had brought out a different horse which belonged to him and the best bit was that he'd blotted out its white star with some boot polish so it looked exactly like Terence. Of all the conniving tricks! So Rocky had been right all along, he hadn't been imagining it.

"Well, of all the dirty, underhand, scheming . . ." Ross fumed.

"Don't I just know it," Rocky agreed.

"Let's call the police," Katie suggested, but Rocky said it was out of the question.

"For one thing we have no proof, it's just our word against theirs."

Hannah refused to testify in court any of what she had told Rocky. It would give her a bad name in racing and no one would employ her. It was all so amazing I felt as if my head was going to blow off my shoulders. In fact, the whole last few days had been pretty spectacular. What with Dancer and Colorado's looming trip to Olympia and a famous rock star staying at Hollywell, I was on tenterhooks about what was going to happen next.

"I've been taken for a right mug," Rocky said, sounding really angry. "But not for much longer. I'm going to find poor Terence if it kills me."

And then Rocky told us in every detail exactly what he planned to do. It was daring... dangerous... But it might just work!

Chapter Six

The next morning Rocky came downstairs looking like death. He kept pointing at his throat and then scribbled a message on a piece of paper.

"I can't talk!"

This was serious. Rocky had lost his voice! What about the concert?

Sarah prodded around in the back of his throat with a spoon and said it looked like laryngitis. Rocky kept writing messages which nobody could understand and then Katie looked up from her bowl of cereal and suggested we call a doctor.

"Good thinking," Sarah said, and then tried to find the doctor's number which she thought was in her diary. We searched everywhere before we eventually found it hidden under Katie's pony magazine.

A roly-poly doctor with tiny little glasses and a big black bag eventually turned up to examine Rocky. He said that Rocky was very rundown and exhausted and his voice had disappeared from too much singing. Katie asked if it would ever come back again. The doctor said that Rocky had to stay in bed and drink lots of fluids and eat wholesome food. Katie said Rocky was always eating chips and hamburgers which the doc banned from then on.

Rocky sat propped up in bed with Matilda on his knee and his hair stuck on end as if it had been brushed with a pitchfork. He scribbled a message which I just managed to read. It said, "Help, get me out of here!"

I stuck a grape in his mouth and told him to be a good patient.

Outside everything was chaotic. Blake was charging around trying to get everything organized for Olympia – he was due to leave in one hour's time and he hadn't even begun to pack his own things.

Colorado was having a lift with a lady who ran a show pony stud a few miles away and her prize stallion was taking part in the best-ridden class. She had a huge horsebox and was quite happy to give Blake and Colorado a lift.

"Where's the sweat rug disappeared to?" Blake shouted nervously, flinging rugs all over the tackroom.

"I've oiled his hooves," Katie said, clutching a tin of hoof oil which was dripping all over her wellies.

"I'll sort this out," I insisted to Blake. "You go in the house and pack!"

Luckily the horsebox was held up in traffic and rolled into the yard half an hour late. With all the drama over Dancer we had left everything to the last minute. Ross rushed out of the house carrying Blake's show-jumping jacket wrapped up in see-through plastic. It was all starting to happen. Blake really was going to Olympia.

Colorado was bandaged up with gamgee sticking out of the tops of his knees and wearing his new pair of hock boots and a beautiful green and beige rug which had his name written down one side and Blake's initials in the corner. Mr Sullivan had bought it especially for his trip to Olympia. He looked every inch a superstar which was a good job because he was going to be rubbing shoulders with some of the best horses in the country.

"I'll answer it!" Sarah shrieked, racing back to the house like a whippet to answer the telephone.

Ross led Colorado up the ramp of the horsebox and he went straight in first time. I think Colorado knew that something special was happening.

I dived back in the house to fetch Blake's leather boots and bumped slap bang into Sarah who got an almighty clout on the forehead.

"That was Rocky's manager," she panted.

Miracle has shot up to number 3 in the charts!"

"*Miracle* is at number 3!" I yelled to Ross who was straining to put up the horsebox ramp.

"Number 3!" Ross shouted to Katie who was searching for the boot polish in the bottom of the grooming box.

"Hadn't somebody better tell Rocky?" I said as a sudden afterthought.

Rocky was delighted and wrote on the back of an envelope, "Blinkin' brilliant!" He'd been scribbling away with a Biro all morning and Sarah said he was writing a song.

Blake finally set off, trundling down the drive, perched in the huge horsebox cab, with Colorado stamping noisily in the back.

"Good luck," Katie shouted, but the lorry engine drowned out her voice, so we just watched until the cream and red Lambourn disappeared down the road out of sight.

"The next time we see them will probably be in the collecting ring," Ross said, as we turned back to the house. "That reminds me, hadn't somebody better check the booking for our coach?"

The coach was due to arrive at seven a.m. the day after tomorrow. Talk about an early start! The concert was the night before, which wouldn't leave much time for a good night's sleep – and the concert was tomorrow night! I kept forgetting – I couldn't believe it had come round so fast! Blake was leaving two days early so that Colorado would have lots of time to adjust to the new environment. He hadn't been to many shows and we wanted to give him the best possible chance to do well. Mr Sullivan was footing the bill as it had been his idea. Just about the whole village was turning out and Sarah had even made a special banner saying "COME ON, BLAKE AND COLORADO". It wouldn't surprise me if we were the noisiest coachload of supporters at the show – probably in the show's whole history.

"Wouldn't it be awful if something went wrong," Katie said. And I couldn't help wondering why nothing ever seemed to run smoothly.

Rocky's manager insisted that he drink nothing but champagne and guzzle spoonfuls of honey. Sarah said that lozenges would work just as well for a fraction of the cost.

It wasn't long before Rocky got bored staying in bed and decided to get up to do the washing up. Sarah said he was the worst patient ever and locked herself away in the study to work on her novel. Ross, Katie and I sorted out the ponies and put extra blankets under their rugs. It was going to be a cold night.

Later, when Rocky was busy toasting teacakes he passed me a message written on a sheet of kitchen roll. "It's still on for tonight."

Sarah thought it was madness but Rocky insisted he had to go through with the plan. Sarah finally admitted that it was the only way to save poor Terence. Sarah made the all-important telephone call on Rocky's behalf and everything was set up for that night.

By 5 o'clock we were all getting anxious.

Sarah took Ross and myself aside while Rocky was watching a Walt Disney film with Katie and Danny.

"No heroics," she said. "I don't want either of you getting hurt." There was no mistaking the serious undertone in her voice. "These guys are dangerous," she said. "They mean business."

By 6 o'clock we were all grouped around the television waiting for Rocky's concert performance to be shown on Channel Four.

"It's you!" Danny shrieked as the cameras zoomed in on Rocky singing. Danny could hardly believe that he was watching a rock star on television and that same person just happened to be sitting next to him on the settee.

The audience were singing along to *Miracle* and one of the fans ran up on to the stage and had to be towed away by two minders.

"I love your suit," Ross said, admiring Rocky's all-in-one sequinned catsuit which made him look thinner than ever. Sarah said he reminded her of Gary Glitter and I joked that Gary Glitter was probably a few years younger!

"I look hideous," Rocky wrote, obviously hating watching himself on television. "And look at that camera angle – it zooms straight in on my double chin!"

"Where's the popcorn?" Katie asked, fishing under the settee.

Sarah had gone out of the room and I decided to follow her.

She had suddenly turned very quiet and I had a distinct feeling something was wrong. I found her in the kitchen attacking a dirty saucepan with a Brillo pad and that was a sure sign that something was up.

"It's nothing," she said, trying to avoid my eyes. "It's stupid, I'm just being silly."

"Tell me," I said. "It's something to do with Rocky, isn't it?"

"No . . . Yes . . . Partly." Sarah flung down the Brillo pad and turned round from the sink.

"When I was eighteen," she said. "I fell in love with a musician. We got engaged. He made the big time and suddenly I wasn't good enough. He dumped me and three weeks later it was in the papers that he was marrying someone else. He was called Marcus and Rocky reminds me so much of him, it brings back bad memories."

"Is that why you didn't like Rocky in the beginning?" I asked.

"Absolutely," Sarah said. "But I decided I didn't like him before I'd even met him and that was wrong. If there's one lesson to be learnt from this, Mel, it's never judge a book by its cover."

"I think he's lonely," I said, referring to Rocky.

Sarah thought for a moment and then put her arm round my shoulder. "You know, Mel," she went on. "I think you could be right."

By seven p.m. we were ready to put our grand plan into action. If we were ever to save Terence it was now or never.

"OK, let's do it," Rocky scribbled on his notepad.

And we set off on an hour's journey to a racecourse.

I had never been to a racecourse before and certainly not at this time of night when it would all be locked up. Tom Richards was stabling the bay thoroughbred at the course overnight so that he'd be as fresh as a daisy in the morning. He was entered for a novice hurdle race but it was what Richards planned to do in the next few hours which interested us most. And no matter what, we had to catch him red-handed.

When we pulled up in the car park there was nobody in sight. We skirted round the back of the grandstand towards a building marked secretary's office. It was in total darkness.

"We're right on time," Ross whispered as Rocky closed his hand round the door handle and eased it open.

"Rocky, is that you?" someone hissed as we crept into the office.

A cigarette lighter flickered in the corner and then a man with a huge beard and moustache fumbled across to us.

"Turn off the torch," he said, as Rocky shone it full in his face. "I don't want anyone knowing I'm here."

The man was called Reg and he was the manager of the racecourse. He was going to act as our star witness.

"Is it all going to plan?" Ross asked, itching to get on with the job.

"Hunky dory," Reg said. "Follow me."

Reg was a fan of Rocky's and when Rocky told him about our dilemma he was the first to say he would help. It was a definite advantage to have the manager on our side.

"Over here," Reg whispered, as we picked our

way through the grass towards the stabling area.

Ross did all the talking because Rocky still hadn't regained his voice. The concert was now looking in serious jeopardy.

"We want to be in box sixty-nine," Reg said, referring to the number of the stable. "Richards' horse is in sixty-eight."

Reg was carrying a walkie-talkie which suddenly crackled into life.

"Still no sign," I heard a woman's voice say from the other end.

"OK, Sue, keep me posted," Reg answered, "Over and out.

"I hope this works," Reg said, as we all hid out of sight in the stable. The bay thoroughbred was next door, noisily munching at his haynet.

Reg complained that he couldn't smoke his pipe, while I immediately froze into one solid ice block. Ross jogged on the spot to keep warm and accidentally trod on Rocky's toe in the dark.

"Sue, come in, Sue – any sign?" Reg was back on the walkie-talkie. The same female voice came through loud and clear.

"No sign yet, Reg, still in position. Over and out."

"Where are they?" Reg said impatiently, more to himself than anyone in particular.

We were waiting for Tom Richards and his

jockey Colin Jensen. Reg's wife, Sue, was sitting in her car at the entrance to the racecourse complete with her walkie-talkie. Her job was to report back to us as soon as she saw anything but to stay well out of sight.

"I spy with my little eye," Reg said, trying to keep us all in good spirits and slapping Rocky on the back.

"You realize we could be here all night."

And that was the one thing none of us wanted to hear. We only had a rough idea as to what time Richards and Jensen planned to make their move. Hannah had tipped off Rocky with as much as she could find out. She had overheard the two of them talking in the feed room and it wasn't good. They were planning on injecting the bay thoroughbred with drugs to make sure that he won. They were both going to lay a lot of money out on a big bet and it was vital that he came in first. The odds would be 100–1 against Terence winning because he had never shown any form in the past. If Richards could get him first past the winning post, he and Jensen would stand to make a lot of money.

And nor was it the first time they had bent the rules. Hannah said they frequently kept horses from drinking water for days and then let them guzzle gallons just before the race. It slowed them down as good as reins. Then when the odds were right they let them win, but now they were using drugs to be extra sure.

We had to catch them.

"Now remember what we discussed," Reg said, apparently enjoying himself. "We can't make a move too early. Let them get into the stable, and we'll nab them as soon as they bring out the syringe. And remember folks, leave Richards to me, I've been after that crooked rogue for years."

It was hard to believe that the man we had met at the racing stables was so corrupt. He had seemed perfectly ordinary, but then it is often said that it's the ones you least expect who turn out to be the villains. Hannah said that Richards had become an alcoholic since his wife died, and since she had been the driving force behind his success as a trainer he couldn't cope without her. I only had to think of Dancer though and my heart hardened. I couldn't even use ignorance as an excuse since he knew exactly what he was doing.

"What was that?" Reg whispered as a voice shouted from somewhere further up the row of boxes, but it was only the stable guard who had gone back to his car to fetch some more beers. I was watching through a gap in the doorframe.

When horses are stabled overnight at a racecourse there is always both a stable guard and the stable manager on duty to prevent any underhand goings on, like Tom Richards was planning. But Reg had decided not to tell his staff what was going on because he was not entirely sure that they weren't involved. It wouldn't be the first time that a stable guard had been bribed with money to turn a blind eye. Reg wanted to see what they were up to which was why everything was top secret and we were all hiding in a cold draughty stable with our feet frozen to the floor.

The stable guard went back into the office with a pack of beers, not once thinking to check the horses. We could hear the television blaring out and Reg bet his next week's wages that they hadn't bothered to look in the stables all night.

"A football team could break in here and they wouldn't notice," Reg fumed, determined to give them both the sack in the morning.

"Sssssh," Ross whispered, terrified that we might blow our cover.

Directly opposite a horse's head looked over the stable door, its ears pricked forward listening.

"That's the favourite," Reg said. "Richards' horse doesn't stand a chance against that."

Suddenly the walkie-talkie crackled noisily and we could hear Sue's voice. Reg nearly dropped it in his excitement.

"They're here," Sue shrieked. "They've just sneaked in through a hole in the wire fencing.

They've brought their own wire cutters, can you believe it?"

For the first time ever I was really scared. Sarah was right, these guys meant business. Nothing was going to stand in their way.

We leaned back as far out of sight as we could and waited.

"Nobody make a noise," Reg said, breathing down my neck like a steam train. "Have you got the baseball bat?" he said to Rocky who was clutching a long wooden bat which Sarah had insisted we take with us. Rocky nodded his head.

"Not long now," Reg whispered, and thirty seconds later, "Where on earth are they?"

I peered through the crack in the doorframe and nearly died with shock. There were two shadows sliding along the opposite row of stables towards the favourite's box.

"We've got the wrong horse," I croaked in horror.

"I don't believe it," Reg hissed. "They're going to nobble the favourite!"

We spilled out of the stable door like a bunch of amateur sleuths, none of us knowing what we were going to do.

"I'll grab Richards," Reg yelled, hurtling towards one of the shadows with his fists clenched tight. Rocky went after the jockey who was already making a run for it. Ross went to Reg's aid who had fallen back from a punch on the nose.

"Hold his arm," Reg yelled as Ross lunged at the slippery trainer.

"Ouch! He bit me!" Ross howled as Tom Richards scrabbled to escape.

"Catch him," Reg shouted to Rocky, his nose dripping with blood. Rocky threw himself at the jockey's legs in a rugby tackle and they both went down together.

"Help!" I yelled as the stable guard and manager came running out of their office.

Rocky was rolling over and over on the ground, desperately trying to get a grip on Jensen.

"Gotcha!" Reg bawled when Ross finally managed to pin back both of Richards' arms behind his back.

Rocky was on his feet and Jensen was looming towards him with the baseball bat clenched in both hands.

"Rocky, watch out!" I shouted.

By this stage my heart was in my mouth and my legs felt like planks of wood. "Do something!" I yelled at the stable guard who was just standing there, gaping like a fish.

Colin Jensen rammed the baseball bat into Rocky's side with every ounze of strength he could muster. I winced in shock and fear.

Rocky toppled over, light as a ragdoll, and lay crumpled in a heap, gasping for breath.

That was when the stable guard finally realized what was going on and leapt on Jensen, knocking him out with one blow.

Reg undid his belt and tied Richards' hands behind his back and before any of us could recover a police siren came screeching on to the racecourse and two policemen rushed to our aid.

"It's all over," Reg gasped, his nose already swelling up like a mountain on his face.

Rocky was still rolling around badly winded and Ross was trying to get him on his feet.

"I think this is what it's all about," Reg said, fishing into Richards' pocket and pulling out a hypodermic syringe.

"Can someone tell me what's been going on?" the oldest policeman said, opening up his black notebook.

"I really think we ought to get Rocky to hospital," I said, fully aware that Rocky had turned pea green.

Realization filtered into the police officer's face. "You're the rock star, aren't you?" he said, getting all excited.

Rocky nodded his head as best he could and leaned even more heavily on Ross's shoulder.

"I wonder if I can have your autograph," he

went on. "It's for the Mrs, of course." The police-man held out his little black book.

"For goodness sake," Rocky boomed in a deep throaty voice.

"Rocky, you've got your voice back," I yelled, delighted.

Rocky grunted and swayed to one side.

"Yes, but I've only blinkin' well cracked my ribs," he bawled, and then fainted as the pain flooded through him.

"Oh, dear," the police officer said.

Chapter Seven

"The show must go on," Rocky insisted, lying on a hospital bed with a doctor attempting to examine him.

"I've done concerts with dislocated shoulders, never mind cracked ribs," Rocky gasped, looking about to pass out again as the doctor felt at his chest.

"Lie back and take deep breaths," Sarah said, who had rushed to the hospital with Danny and Katie as soon as I rang her from the pay phone.

"That makes it hurt even more," Rocky croaked.

"Well, just keep quiet then."

We had rushed Rocky to casualty in the back of the police car with the siren going and Rocky wrapped up in the police officer's jacket because he was trembling like a leaf. Rocky had given them free tickets to the concert by way of a thank-you but we all seriously doubted that he would be fit enough to perform.

"It's not as bad as I thought," the doctor said, coming back with the X-ray results, and looking

77

at Rocky over the tops of his spectacles. "You've just fractured a couple of ribs," he said, "but they'll soon knit together. You're a lucky man, Mr – er – Rocky."

"And that's all?" Katie said when the doctor had disappeared. "Just painkillers, not even a bandage?"

The doctor had said that nowadays they just left ribs to heal by themselves. I must admit it all seemed a bit of an anti-climax.

The nurses had put Rocky in a private cubicle as soon as he came in so he wouldn't be recognized by the waiting patients. But word was quickly getting round that somebody famous was in the ward and the nurses had already had to restrain two teenage girls who had broken through the security.

"It's Rocky," a youth yelled, with a stud through his nose and a sling on his arm. He'd just sneaked up without anyone noticing and yanked back the curtain on Rocky's cubicle.

"I think it's time for a quick exit," Rocky said, grabbing his painkillers and about to leg it.

"Rocky, Rocky!" three women shouted, running along the corridor in hospital gowns with their arms outstretched.

"This way," the nurse said, pushing Rocky and the rest of us through a door and locking it behind her. "You're enough to set off a stampede," she said, flushing pink in the face.

She threw a white sheet over Rocky's head so nobody would recognize him and we dragged him out into the car park and towards our car.

"Crikey, that was close," Rocky gasped, pulling off the sheet and chewing on a painkiller for instant relief.

"What time is it?" Rocky said, fighting with his seat belt which kept getting stuck.

"Half past two in the morning," Katie stated, looking at her Mickey Mouse watch under the interior light. "We've got precisely seventeen hours until the concert," she added, counting up on her fingers.

"Roll on the curtain call," Rocky shouted, leaning back against the seat looking desperately weak.

"Of all the nasty, cruel, insensitive people," Ross fumed as James gave us the lowdown on Tom Richards and Colin Jensen.

When we had left them they were squabbling like children with Jensen blaming it all on Richards and vice versa. They were taken away for questioning in another police car and we left Reg to do the explaining on our behalf.

James told us how they had planned to inject

the favourite with a massive dose of a drug called
A.C.P. The horse was sure to be called in for a
drug test and then disqualified from the race.
Apparently this was one of the best ways to fix a
race and discredit another trainer.

"They won't be getting up to any more tricks
though," James said. "The Jockey Club will see to
that. In fact, I shouldn't think Richards will ever
get a licence again, or Jensen any rides for that
matter."

The Jockey Club was the ruling organization of
racing and had enormous power.

"So in our own small way we've done everyone
a favour," I said.

"Hollywell to the rescue yet again," Sarah joked.

By late afternoon we were all in a state of high
tension. Even Rocky's manager had driven up
especially from London and was skittering around
like a cat on hot bricks making everyone nervous.

"Queenie's got too many plaits," Danny
shouted, frantically running into the house.

We had told Danny and Katie to polish up
Queenie because there was going to be a surprise.
Danny's eyes had grown as wide as saucers but we
all refused to tell them what the surprise was.

"I've had an accident," Katie came in after

Danny, holding up one of Queenie's plaits in one hand and a pair of scissors in the other.

"Katie!" we all shrieked.

She'd lopped off Queenie's forelock!

"No, we can't stick it back on," I yelled, looking at Queenie's golf ball plaits and the short stub between her ears which was once her forelock. "I knew you couldn't be trusted," I yelled at Katie.

"Peace and goodwill to all men," Rocky chimed from behind me just as I was about to throttle my little sister.

A car-load of musicians turned up just hours before they were due on stage with tinsel draped all round the windows.

"Merry Christmas!" they cried, spilling out into the yard and all wearing identical "The Return" leather jackets.

"Meet the band!" Rocky shouted, slapping the youngest one on the back and then wincing from the sudden movement. Rocky had taken so many painkillers it was amazing he could still stand up.

Blake rang up to say that he'd arrived at Olympia safe and well and Colorado was eating twice as much as the other horses even though he was only half their size.

Despite police questioning, neither Richards nor

Jensen had admitted to kidnapping Rocky's real horse. But the police firmly believed our side of the story, especially after Rocky showed them the bay thoroughbred's forehead and how its small white star had been blotted out with boot polish. It was amazing that Richards and Jensen had been able to get away with it.

The police said they were questioning previous owners who had kept their horses at Richards' yard and all sorts of underhand activities were coming to light. But where was Terence? Somewhere there was a beautiful, vulnerable thoroughbred in need of our help and we couldn't find him!

"Mel, are you going to get ready?" Sarah shouted from upstairs as she dressed for the concert.

Ross had gone with Rocky to the village hall to act as his valet, in other words to help him get dressed and on to the stage without mishap. I'm sure Rocky was so experienced he could do it with his eyes closed but I didn't say anything to Ross. Besides, it was Rocky's idea.

I was still covered in Queenie's hairs and the grease from her winter coat and if I didn't get changed soon, people would think I was a horse. I certainly smelt like one.

"Katie, you little rat!" I yelled, as she slammed the bathroom door shut in my face.

The village hall was totally transformed. I had never seen anything quite like it. There were people and cars everywhere, and the police were trying to direct traffic in one direction while everyone insisted on going in another. Girls were shrieking their heads off.

I couldn't understand what all the fuss was about. After all, Rocky was just an ordinary person. Even Danny wasn't so star-struck since he found out that Rocky's white streak came straight out of a peroxide bottle.

"What you see is not always what you get," Rocky had said, wagging his finger while showing Danny how to put on stage make-up. Being a rock-star wasn't half as glamorous as I'd first thought. In fact it was extremely hard work.

Normally with famous bands they have another singer who goes on stage first to "warm up" the audience. This time, however, because it was a special event, Rocky was going straight on. The rest of the band came on first and started playing their instruments, just getting into the mood and building up the excitement before Rocky made his appearance.

We were all worried sick in case Rocky collapsed during the performance. Nobody knew he had fractured his ribs, apart from the other band members. Rocky was going to take his painkillers half an hour beforehand and literally hope for the best. The drummer, who had spiky blond hair, promised to keep a special eye on him.

"Rocky won't let you down," he said, and really meant it.

Sarah, James, Katie and myself had seats reserved at the front of the hall in the far left-hand corner. We could see everything from there, including what was happening in the wings. Ross gave me a wave from where he was helping the drummer on with his jacket.

I was already tingling with excitement. People were pouring in, looking up and down for their seats and chattering away nineteen to the dozen. I recognized loads of people from school and the local Pony Club. I'd never been to a concert before so it was a whole new experience.

Rocky's manager was on stage wearing a multi-coloured suit and talking on the microphone. I blushed the colour of beetroot when he mentioned all our names and told everyone about the import-ance of places like Hollywell Stables. Everyone started clapping and I didn't know where to look. There was a television camera directed straight at us and Katie had the nerve to wave.

There was a massive drum roll and then Rocky came running out on to the stage clapping his hands together above his head and looking sensational. He was wearing a white suit with glitter and gold stars all over it. He launched straight into a really upbeat song, leaping around stage from one end to the other and blasting out the words in his powerful voice. How was he going to keep this up for the next two hours?

It was brilliant. The music just flowed on and on. Everyone was enjoying it, even the older people and the very young. It was loud and energetic but you could understand the words and there was a definite rhythm.

"Rocky for ever!" someone shouted out from the back and then somebody gave a wolf whistle. Another person threw a rose on to the stage and I realized it was our next-door neighbour. She was jiving around in her seat and I knew for a fact that she was over sixty.

Rocky then sang *Miracle* and everybody joined in, swaying in their seats, belting out the lyrics, "Miracles do happen, never give in."

I caught sight of Ross in the wings holding on to a towel waiting for the interval. Rocky was beginning to look tired but I don't think anybody else noticed. When he went off to change outfits the audience were going mad, cheering for more. The stage was littered with flowers and still more were being thrown in the air.

When Rocky leapt back on stage wearing black

and gold, the audience were on their feet. After Rocky had been through all his hit songs he put on a long white beard and started singing *Jingle Bells* and *We Wish You a Merry Christmas*. It was fantastic. It took him ages to get everybody settled down so he could talk into the mike.

Rocky wished everyone a Happy Christmas and then said something which brought a lump to my throat.

"I want to introduce you to a very special lady," he said. "Someone who means a great deal to a lot of people."

And then out of the wings, reluctantly at first, Queenie stepped on to the stage, her gentle dusky eyes taking everything in and Danny by her side, clutching on to her brand new headcollar and grinning from ear to ear. Rocky lifted Danny on to Queenie's back and then led her out into the front of the stage. She didn't hesitate once, and looked as if she was enjoying every minute of it.

All the audience had hushed as Rocky told them Queenie's story. There wasn't a dry eye in the house when he had finished and even Sarah had to borrow James' big white hanky. I had never felt more proud of Hollywell Stables than at that moment.

Rocky launched into his final song and leaned on Queenie's neck for support. Queenie didn't mind a bit and I suspected she sensed that Rocky was in a lot of pain. We all knew that Queenie's hearing was not one hundred per cent; it had deteriorated in the short time we'd owned her. But now with all the music and clapping from the audience it was a blessing in disguise. Danny had always said that Queenie smiled like a human being when she was happy and at that moment I could see what he meant. She was beaming.

Rocky had to come back on stage three times to a standing ovation before everybody started to file out of the hall. The concert had been a massive success and everyone was leaving donations at the door. Two girls came up to me and promised to do a sponsored swim to raise money, and one old lady gave me a beautiful gold brooch which I reluctantly said I couldn't possibly accept.

It seemed everybody had been touched by the whole occasion and I felt as if my head was in the clouds. If I'd have stepped outside and seen Father Christmas flying through the sky on his sleigh I wouldn't have been at all surprised.

"Mel, come on!" James yelled, yanking at my sweater and dragging me forward. "Rocky's collapsed backstage."

We all ran like mad to where Ross was pushing Rocky in a wheelchair out of the back doors. There were people everywhere and cameras clicking. I was terrified we were going to get crushed.

"Get him in the car!" Rocky's manager shouted, trying to make a path through the sea of people.

We fell into the back of the limousine in a heap and Rocky was clutching his sides and gasping for breath.

"Where're my tablets?" he said, and then passed out on Ross's shoulder.

When we got home Rocky had come round and was looking a lot better. The phone was going mad with newspaper reporters wanting to do interviews and fans ringing up to congratulate us. I felt exhausted so I dreaded to think how Rocky must have felt.

"Anyone for bacon and eggs?" Sarah asked, brandishing the frying pan and picking up a couple of eggs. Sarah was immensely proud of our fresh eggs and she'd actually managed to get our chickens laying all year round by playing them Radio One in the mornings. Sarah swore that it worked despite James's reservations.

"Count me in," Rocky's manager chirped up, volunteering to help with the cooking.

"Do you realize it's Olympia tomorrow?" Katie said, yawning as wide as the Channel tunnel.

"Rocky's got something to tell you about that,"

his manager said, grinning over the frying pan almost gleefully.

"Oh, yes?" Sarah said, looking curious.

Rocky was supposed to be leaving for Glasgow that night to do a television show which meant he would miss Olympia. We were all disappointed but it couldn't be helped.

"The show's been cancelled," Rocky's manager said, snipping at the bacon. "Rocky, tell them what's going on and put them out of their misery."

"Well," Rocky started, trying to act really serious. "*I'm going with you!*"

Chapter Eight

The next morning we were all staggering around, exhausted, with our eyes practically propped open with matchsticks.

I'd forgotten to set my alarm clock which meant we were all up late, and to make matters worse, the coach had just arrived in the yard fifteen minutes early. Already people were swarming up the drive and piling on to the coach.

"Where's my wig gone?" Rocky asked, swilling back some black coffee which looked revolting.

"Last seen in Jigsaw's basket," Ross joked, flying out to the stables to finish feeding the horses.

"Where's the orange juice?" Katie said, trailing around in her pyjamas.

"Look, will you all just get a move on," Sarah shrieked, spilling hot tea everywhere as she frantically filled up the Thermos flasks.

"Everybody's waiting to go and we're not even dressed. Rocky, do something!"

Rocky swallowed a painkiller and then strutted into action.

Katie was packed off upstairs to get dressed and I was ordered to help Ross with the horses. Rocky decided to tackle the Pony Club lot who were charging round the stables and scaring Bluey and Sophie to death.

Sarah bungled out of the house with an armload of coats saying that it was going to be freezing cold and one little boy with red hair and glasses was actually taking bets on whether it was going to snow.

Rocky eventually found his wig behind the fridge and put on his dark glasses which looked ridiculous in the middle of winter. He was determined not to be recognized; considering what happened at the hospital, that was probably good sense.

I went to check on Dancer for the umpteenth time, even though one of the Pony Club instructors was going to stay and baby-sit the horses with Jigsaw who couldn't understand why he wasn't going too.

"Mel, will you hurry up!" Rocky shouted, hopping on the spot as the coachdriver revved up his engine.

"That's everybody," Sarah said, shouting out the last name on her clipboard. It was like being at school.

We were just about to close the coach doors

when a car screamed up the drive, puffing blue smoke, and Rocky's band leapt out of the doors, all wearing Santa hats and insisting they were coming with us.

"Is that it now?" the coach driver shouted, looking slightly bewildered.

"Olympia, here we come!" Rocky yelled, and we finally lurched out of the drive heading for the motorway to London.

"Isn't this exciting?" a lady wearing a pom-pom hat shrieked who was sitting next to me and telling me all about her job as a secretary.

Rocky was having his ear chewed off by a Sergeant Major sort of man who was discussing the meaning of life.

"I want to go to the toilet," a little girl whined from the back and her mother told her to cross her legs and keep quiet.

We'd just stopped off at a motorway service centre where everybody had queued up for the loos and we'd lost three teenage boys who we eventually found chatting to a team of football players who they insisted were playing for England.

"You realize we're nearly an hour late," Sarah whispered to me as she handed out the tickets for the show.

"Look, it's snowing!" the little boy with the red

hair and glasses shouted. "You owe me ten pence," he said to the boy sitting next to him, holding out his hand.

Huge, heavy snowflakes splatted against the windows and outside everything looked a white haze.

"It's coming down a bit fast," Ross said to me, and I couldn't decide whether I was pleased or worried.

"We've got to get back tonight, remember," Ross added, and I suddenly wished it was summer.

"Seventy-two miles to London," someone shouted, and then there was choruses of *I'm Dreaming of a White Christmas* from the back of the coach.

"What's that noise?" Ross said, as a funny droning sound started up from the engine.

It felt as if we were losing power.

"Don't say we're going to break down," Sarah said, looking panic-stricken.

We were already late and Blake was competing at three o'clock.

The coach pulled to a sorry halt on the hard shoulder and then the engine puttered out altogether. This was the last thing we needed. Help! I felt like screaming.

"Just a temporary hitch," the coach driver

assured us, chewing his nails and not looking very convincing.

Rocky immediately took charge and hammered out loads of phone numbers on his mobile telephone and impressed everybody with his quick thinking.

Sarah whispered in my ear that it looked serious. The coach driver said he couldn't repair the engine and there were no other coaches in the depot. It would take ages for them to reach us with another vehicle. All we could do in the meantime was just sit there.

And that's what we did for the next hour and ten minutes.

"Look!" someone shouted, pointing frantically at a black and gold coach which had just slushed on to the hard shoulder in front of us.

Down the side of the coach, written in gold was the words "Rocky – The Return". It was only Rocky's tour coach!

Everybody was on their feet, shouting and applauding, thumping Rocky on the back which did nothing for his fractured ribs.

"How did you fix it?" Ross shouted to Rocky above all the commotion.

"So much for keeping a low profile!" I yelled, unable to stop grinning from sheer relief.

"Hey, a man's gotta do what a man's gotta do,"

Rocky twanged, putting on a funny voice and winking at us both.

"Come on, everybody!" Sarah blasted, leading the way to the open doors. "It's time to jump ship!"

We passed through London in a state of awe. The Christmas decorations were like nothing I'd ever seen and together with the backdrop of falling snow they looked magical. Katie had her nose pressed to the window, gazing at all the famous shops and restaurants. But the best moment was seeing the front entrance to Olympia. I never expected it to look so grand. My stomach curled up in a knot just from the excitement. Everybody was buzzing with anticipation, and I tried to remember each little detail of everything that happened, just like you do when you want to cherish something forever.

"You all right, Mel?" Ross said. And then he propped me up under his arm and we stepped out into the snow and straight into Olympia.

Chapter Nine

"Where have you been?" Blake shouted, looking desperate.

We were picking our way across the outdoor warm-up ring towards Blake who was leading Colorado around and fighting to keep him under control.

There were horses and grooms everywhere, and I was sure I caught sight of John Whitaker riding past on a big chestnut horse.

"What's wrong with him?" I asked, stroking Colorado's neck which was already damp with sweat. He was plunging at the sand with his forelegs and snorting like a wild stallion.

"He thinks he's back on the prairies," Sarah joked, and she wasn't far wrong.

"How am I going to make him concentrate like this?"

Usually Blake was as cool as a cucumber but when he won the qualifying class in the summer there was no pressure – he had nothing to lose. Now his whole future was hanging in the balance.

"Don't panic!" Rocky spoke up behind us, looking ridiculous in his blond wig and dark glasses.

"How did you get in here?" we all shouted together.

The rules were very strict about who was allowed behind the scenes and we'd all been sent special badges to wear around the stables and collecting rings.

"I 'ave my special ways," Rocky grinned, and I had a distinct feeling he wasn't telling us the full story. There was another Rocky surprise brewing.

"Out of my way," a girl yelled, thundering past on a big grey horse towards the main arena.

"Manners, manners," Rocky tutted, and Ross pulled a face behind the girl's back.

The Newcomers' class was well underway but Blake was one of the last to go so there was quite a while to wait.

Blake decided to ride Colorado round to calm him down and I goggled at all the famous riders who were waiting for the next class, milling around in chaps and jackets with their sponsor's name on the back.

"Mel!" Sarah shrieked, grabbing hold of my arm and trying to talk out of the corner of her mouth. "Over there – it's Franke Sloothaak!"

A handsome-looking man rode past on a beautiful Hanoverian. He smiled at Sarah and I had to stop her chasing after him. Franke Sloothaak was one of the best riders in the world and also one of the most popular.

I caught sight of Rocky near some practice jumps, chatting to two girls who wanted his autograph.

"The disguise didn't work then?" I teased when he rejoined us.

"Sure did," Rocky answered, looking smug. "They thought I was a famous showjumper!"

Ross stayed with Blake while we moved towards the main arena to take a look at the course. Blake had just told us the real reason why he was so nervous. The second-to-last fence was a nasty looking upright made up of planks with a huge yellow circle in the middle – Colorado's favourite colour.

"You've got to think positive," I had told Blake.

"It's all mind over matter," Rocky insisted, but Blake had already resigned himself to losing.

"So much for Mr Sullivan's offer," he said. "There's no way we're going to get in the placings now."

Poor Blake, he was devastated. And when I saw the planks I could understand why. They were awesome. They were positioned straight off a tight corner and partly hidden by another jump so that horse and rider wouldn't see them properly until the last few strides. Planks were always difficult to jump at the best of times because they were so upright and horses found it hard to judge their take-off. But these looked near impossible.

The girl on the grey horse had just come out of the ring with a clear round but she didn't look very happy about it.

"That's Fiona Cunningham," I whispered to Sarah. She was the youngest daughter of a really famous showjumping family and I'd read in a pony magazine that she was a brilliant rider but she had an attitude problem. Everybody called her "the brat".

Most of the horses were knocking the planks down and also the last element of the treble. It was two strides to the huge last spread but they were long strides and most of the horses couldn't make the distance. At 14.2 hands Colorado was really going to have his work cut out. Colorado's strength was in his quick turns and twists which he'd learnt as a cow horse. He wasn't very good at lengthening his stride.

"This is not turning out to be our day," Sarah said, and I knew she had been reading my thoughts.

"Where there's life there's hope," I said, trying not to show my true feelings.

"Colorado's special," Rocky said in my ear. "He'll come good, you wait and see."

I remembered a horse which Sarah was always telling me about. A 14.2 pony called Stroller who had gone to the Olympics and won a silver medal. He had proved that size wasn't important, that ponies could be just as brilliant as horses. Colorado still had a chance. Blake just had to believe in him.

Katie and Danny came running up with candy floss stuck all round their mouths and a book stuffed with famous autographs.

"How did you get all these?" Sarah asked, looking amazed.

"Rocky introduced us to one of the riders and he took us into the competitors' box," Katie gasped in excitement.

"Did he now," Sarah said, looking around for Rocky who had conveniently disappeared.

Blake sat on Colorado's back in the famous Olympia tunnel waiting to be called into the main arena. Colorado stood stock still with his ears pricked forward and his beautiful neck arched like a champion. Blake's long legs were wrapped round his sides and as he nudged him to go forward the gates opened and the commentator announced their names.

"This is the first time a wild cow horse has ever taken part at Olympia," the commentator went on. "Half Mustang, half thoroughbred, ladies and gentlemen, and only 14.2 hands."

Colorado stepped proudly out into the main arena, his long mane and tail flying loose and his brown and white coat gleaming under the lights.

"I can't stand skewbalds," a woman gossiped to her friend beside me. "They're so common, don't you think?"

If I wasn't so interested in watching Blake I'd have given her a piece of my mind.

I caught a glimpse of our coachload up in the stands waving their banner, "COME ON, BLAKE AND COLORADO".

Colorado set off in a canter, approaching the first jump which was a simple brush fence. He sailed over and was immediately looking for the next.

At last he had settled down, and the huge audience and indoor arena didn't seem to be bothering him in the least.

Steady, Blake, steady. He was coming into the wall. Those bricks were so easy to push off. Be careful.

Colorado gave it a good two feet, even though

it was a huge jump. But then all the fences were massive. Even though the class was for novice horses it was still extremely tough. Sarah said she could barely watch and I knew how she felt. The planks were looming up. Over the white gate, push on for the parallel. Colorado leapt into the air in a beautiful rounded arch springing off his hocks like a true champion. He reminded me of the great Milton who cleared every jump by miles. Blake sat as quietly as he could, his soft hands following the movement, keeping Colorado balanced.

It is very difficult to stay in perfect harmony with a horse when you are quite tall and the horse only a 14.2 pony! But Blake was a natural. It was like watching Mark Todd and he was one of the best riders ever.

"Mel, he's overshot the planks," Sarah said, clutching at my arm.

Oh, no. Colorado had put such a big jump in at the parallel that he had bounded on too far and now Blake had to bring him to a halt in the far corner and turn him for the planks.

"He'll never do it," Sarah said. "He's broken the rhythm."

"Come on, Blake," Rocky chuntered beside us. "Keep your cool."

Colorado stiffened through his whole body when he saw the planks. Blake pushed him into canter but he was backing off his leg the whole time. Blake squeezed him forward asking the ultimate question. The best horse and rider partnerships were always the ones based on trust. But would Colorado trust Blake enough to jump the yellow planks?

One, two, three. Blake had him on a perfect stride. All Colorado had to do now was lift upwards.

"Come on, Colorado," Sarah yelled, causing the gossipy woman next to us to scowl in distaste.

Colorado did it. He took the chance and thrust himself into the air. It wasn't the neatest of jumps because he was stiff with fear but he cleared the planks and left them standing.

A great whoop went up from high in the stands and I saw Rocky's band on their feet waving and cheering.

Now for the treble. First the upright. One stride to another upright. Blake really pushed on so he would land well out on the other side. The pole rolled but stayed put. Colorado stretched for those next two strides with everything he'd got. It almost appeared to be in slow motion. Colorado was still too short going into the spread.

He put in a massive leap. Later we all joked that he must have got rockets attached to his heels. When Colorado passed through the finish, everybody in the building was clapping like mad. The commentator called it a gutsy performance but more important it was a clear round. Blake was into the jump-off.

"I need the hackamore," Blake said, leaping off Colorado and immediately loosening his girth.

"Is that wise?" Sarah asked, but it was well within the rules to change bridles halfway through the class.

A brown horse came out of the arena with a clear round. That meant there were six clears altogether. Colorado had to go well in the jump-off to be in the places.

"Someone just get me the hackamore, please," Blake said, undoing Colorado's throat lash.

A hackamore was a bitless bridle which worked by putting pressure on the nose. It often made horses more responsive to their riders and, after overshooting the planks, Blake needed more control.

"I'm going to have to turn really sharp to the planks," Blake said, talking about the jump-off.

"Isn't that risky?" I said. "What if he refuses?"

"It's a gamble, Mel, but everything's a gamble. Everything we've done in the last week has been a gamble."

"He who dares, wins," Ross said, coming back

with the hackamore. And even I could see the truth in that.

Fiona Cunningham was the first to go.

"She's sure to go fast," Blake said, watching her intensely, while Ross was leading Colorado round in the collecting ring.

Fiona pushed her massive grey horse through the start and it scorched round, eating up the ground with its long strides. Another clear round.

"We can only beat her on the corners," Blake said. "Colorado can turn quicker, I know he can."

The next two horses each had a fence down which meant they collected four faults and the one after that had a slow clear. Blake had to go clear and fast to get placed.

"Remember, there's still one horse to go after you," Sarah said.

"Just do your best," Rocky said. "Nobody can ask for more than that."

Colorado nodded his head as if in agreement and Blake vaulted up into the saddle.

The atmosphere was electric as Colorado trotted into the arena. He looked so confident and in charge. Determination was written all over his face – there was no way anyone was going to beat him.

As Blake waited for the bell which meant that he could begin his round, Colorado gave a little buck which made the audience laugh. The commentator called him a real showman, but as Blake turned him into the first fence, they were both deadly serious.

They say that horses have a special sixth-sense whereby they pick up their riders' feelings and the importance of an occasion. There was no doubt in my mind that Colorado knew exactly what was at stake.

He was jumping his heart out. Blake turned so quickly into the wall I thought he was going to crash through it. Colorado lifted up from an impossible angle, corkscrewing over the top with just an inch to spare. Push, push, push towards the gate. Colorado leapt into the air a stride early, stretched and landed way out on the other side. The commentator was going crazy with excitement.

"He's two seconds up!" he yelled. "The little fella's in the lead!"

The parallel loomed up big and square. It was a spread with the front and back poles exactly the same height so the horses couldn't judge the width until they were airborne. It wasn't easy, not at the best of times, but Colorado was going flat out. Surely he'd crash into the front rail?

"Blake, you're going too fast!" Sarah shrieked, squeezing my arm in a vice-like grip.

"Steady up!" I said under my breath, my throat dried up with nerves.

Colorado launched into the air with another flying leap.

"Anyone would think he was in the Grand National," the commentator said.

The audience gasped. Colorado's strength was amazing. That jump was enormous but he made it look nothing. He was a horse in a million and everybody watching could see that. You didn't have to know a lot about show-jumping to recognize true greatness.

"Oh, heavens," the commentator gasped.

"Oh, no," we all screamed.

Blake turned Colorado on the spot. Sand flew up in a great spray and Colorado's hindquarters skidded right underneath his body.

"He's gone too far this time," Sarah said. "He'll never do it."

Colorado faced the planks from just one stride out. It was an impossible task. He was practically at a stand still.

"Come on, Colorado!" our supporters yelled, waving their banner, and then the rest of the audience joined in. They were all shouting, "Come on, Colorado!" at the top of their voices.

Colorado knew they were willing him on. He sat down on his hocks and thrust himself upwards, his forelegs folded up tight underneath him so as not to catch the top plank.

"He's done it, he's done it!" I yelled, escstatic.

"But what about the treble?" Sarah said.

They went clear over the first two jumps but then Colorado stumbled going into the last. He'd never get the two strides now. He'd have to refuse!

But Colorado hadn't come this far for nothing. He knew what he had to do. He picked himself up in a split second, pushed his weight back on his haunches and popped in three strides and then somehow still managed to clear the final spread.

The audience went wild.

Sarah was jumping up and down with tears running down her cheeks and I had a lump in my throat the size of a tennis ball.

"Flipping brilliant!" Rocky kept saying over and over, sniffing loudly and pretending he'd got a cold.

Colorado came thundering back up the tunnel like a gymkhana pony. Blake had his arms wrapped round his neck and was patting him non-stop. We all rushed up to congratulate them and Blake slithered out of the saddle saying his knees were trembling.

"*Your* knees are trembling," Sarah bawled. "We can barely stand up!"

*

People came crowding round shaking Blake's hand and patting Colorado.

The last horse had just finished his round but he'd gone for a slow clear and still got four faults. The commentator announced Blake and Colorado as the winners with Fiona Cunningham in second place.

"You've won!" I shrieked, unable to take it all in. Colorado had come to Olympia as an outsider and walked off with the first prize.

"Blake, you've got to go back in," Sarah yelled, as the commentator announced the prizegiving.

A journalist from one of the pony magazines had already collared him and was asking loads of questions.

Colorado waltzed back into the arena as if he was eighteen hands high. He looked so tiny in front of all the other horses but he was the champion, not them. Small but perfectly formed, as Rocky described him.

Fiona Cunningham had stormed off in a tantrum and deliberately missed the prizegiving, which everybody thought was bad form. Blake was presented with a huge trophy and Colorado had two rosettes pinned to his bridle which he tried to eat. It seemed a lifetime since I had sat in Louella's house drooling over her pictures of Olympia – and now here I was behind the scenes and Blake was about to take over her rides on Royal Storm and the Wizard. It was fantastic. And it just proved how quickly life could change, for the better.

Colorado did his lap of honour, throwing in the odd buck to please the crowds. Blake couldn't stop grinning. The audience couldn't stop clapping. Colorado had come to Olympia and taken on the best novice horses in the country and he'd won. It was unbelievable.

As he came trotting out of the arena, Ross threw the beige and green rug over Colorado's quarters and Blake quickly loosened his girth. Sarah unclipped the championship rosettes and handed them to Blake. "I hope these are the first of many," she said.

"They will be!" I added emphatically. And I knew without any doubt that Blake and Colorado were destined to be champions.

Blake and Ross led Colorado off towards the stables, while Katie grabbed hold of Sarah and myself and literally dragged us back through the tunnel where the tractors were moving in to clear the jumps from the arena. "Come on, it's the Shetland Grand National next!"

"Watch out!" Sarah shouted, as two little Shetlands raced past with their riders desperately trying to stop them.

"Aren't they brilliant," Katie shrieked, as one

jockey with pigtails fell off and started crying.

"Do you think we'll ever have any Shetlands?" Danny asked Sarah.

"All things considering, Danny, I think there's a very good chance."

Shetlands were one of the most common breeds of pony to be victims of neglect. It was because they were so small that people bought them without thinking and then had no idea how to look after them.

"We've missed the dressage," I said, looking at the programme and trying to balance everybody's drinks on my knee.

It had been brilliant earlier when Blake was competing but it was nice now to be able to relax and enjoy the rest of the show.

Rocky sat next to me and we made bets on who was going to win the National. Danny was right in the end when a chubby little black one called Desdemona scorched past the finish.

The main show-jumping class was incredible. It was totally different from watching it on television, a million times better because you got all the atmosphere. The jumps had to be seen to be believed but the horses made it look so easy. We all agreed that Franke Sloothaak and John Whitaker were our favourite riders.

It only seemed five minutes until it was time for

the pantomime and then Father Christmas appeared with his sleigh. All the horses piled in for the finale and Sarah was clicking her camera like mad when Blake rode in on Colorado.

"You haven't pulled back the shutter," Katie said, taking over.

"So that's why I couldn't see anything!" Sarah said, looking vague.

"I don't think Joseph would have been chewing bubble gum," I muttered to Rocky, pointing at the nativity scene.

"Where's Rocky?" I shouted when I realized I'd been talking to myself.

"Must have gone for some more food," Katie said, stuffing herself on homemade fudge and peppermint creams.

"He's left his wig and glasses," I said, fishing under the chair.

"Look over there," Sarah pointed towards the orchestra.

"I knew it," I said, puffing with indignation. "I just knew he was up to something."

Rocky was going to sing the opening verse of *The First Noel* and then everybody was going to join in.

He stood on a small platform, holding the mike and sung with such emotion that everybody was enrapt. His voice was so clear and powerful that many critics thought he should have been an opera singer. Personally I thought he was just fine as he was.

"The first Noel the angel did say . . ."

We all joined in and Sarah complained that she didn't know all the words so we both ended up miming. Everyone joined hands to sing *Auld Lang Syne* and the articifial snow came pouring down from high up in the roof. All the riders dropped their reins and linked arms, the horses no doubt thinking they'd all gone mad.

The applause for Rocky was ear-shattering and nobody clapped louder than us. In fact I'd done so much clapping the palms of my hands were throbbing.

Back at the temporary stables, behind the scenes, we all mucked in to settle Colorado down for the night. He wasn't coming home until the following morning, after the Best Ridden Championship. Blake undid his bandages while Sarah filled his water bucket and Ross went off to look for some clean woodshavings. Stabled at the side of Colorado were two police horses that Danny and Katie actually managed to sit on with the groom's consent. They looked like two peas on a drum.

Everywhere people were rushing around tending to their horses, and chattering about the day's events. Rocky had reclaimed his wig and glasses and was busy trying to ring Hollywell on his mobile phone to check that all was well.

"Just what is he doing?" Blake said, as Rocky wandered all over the place trying to get a connection.

The trouble with mobile phones was that sometimes you couldn't get a line and you had to move around until you did which could take forever.

"Wouldn't it have been easier to use the pay phone?" Sarah said, but then Rocky came shrieking across, waving the phone in the air and losing his wig in a pile of horse muck.

"I've got through," he yelled, on the verge of hysteria. "And guess what?" he said, not waiting for us to answer. "They've found Terence!"

Chapter Ten

"It's him!" Rocky said, peering into an old cow-shed which hadn't seen the light of day for years. It was all boarded up and there was no sign of life, let alone a deserted racehorse.

"Where?" I gasped, catching up, out of breath, tingling with excitement at the prospect of finding Terence.

"Over here!" I shouted to James and Ross who were heading in the direction of the barns.

I heard a faint rustle of straw and a snort which sounded like a horse.

"We've found him! We've found Terence!"

Rocky was already trying to find a way into the shed, pulling at a loose sheet of boarding and cutting his hand on a nail.

"It's all right, boy, we'll get you out of there."

"Quick!" I said as James and Ross came running up. "He's in here!"

Together James and Rocky tried to wrench open a door that had been nailed across with planks of wood. We could hear Terence now – he was moving around inside and kicking at the sides of the shed.

"He's OK," Rocky breathed, peering through a hole that he'd made in the door. "Hang on, boy, we'll soon get you out."

Terence neighed then as if he knew we were going to rescue him. I couldn't believe that someone had shut up a horse like this for nearly a week.

We were in an old farmyard, high up on a hill, miles away from any houses. It belonged to Tom Richards' brother who was on holiday abroad and this is where they'd decided to bring Terence.

It had taken ages to find him. When we got back from Olympia we discovered that Tom Richards had sent the police on a wild goose chase. They hadn't found Terence at all. Richards was admitting to nothing and neither was Jensen, although Jensen was spilling the beans about all of Richards' shady dealings in the hope that he'd get off with a lighter sentence.

It was Hannah who had eventually found the address to the farm in Richards' office. She had been asking questions and snooping around for days and it had finally paid off. If it wasn't for Hannah I wondered if we would have ever found Terence.

"We're in!" Rocky shouted, as the door fell open and we walked inside.

It was pitch black and at first I couldn't see a thing. There was a terrible musty, damp smell and the bedding must have been at least two feet deep. I don't think it had been cleaned out for years. There was fungus growing in the corners and dense cobwebs everywhere.

We'd all presumed that Terence must have had the run of the whole shed but when we got inside we discovered that he was partitioned off in a small corner and there was barely room for him to turn around. It was the wooden partition that he'd been kicking at. The first thing I saw was his hindlegs which were peppered with splinters from the wood.

We all fell quiet as our eyes adjusted to the dark and we finally got our first good look at Terence.

"It's been a long time, boy," Rocky whispered, putting up his hand to stroke him, but Terence flinched away terrified. His beautiful bay head was pinched and anxious, full of mistrust.

"How can people do this to a horse?" Rocky said, filled with horror.

But it was a question we'd asked ourselves a million times over and none of us knew the answer.

In the end, James had to sedate Terence in order for us to get him out of the shed. His nerves were totally shredded. It took us half an hour just to get a headcollar on him.

Out in the daylight he blinked frantically after being locked up in the dark for so long. His head was hung low and he was hobbling on three legs.

"Look at this!" James said, probing at a deep wound on Terence's near hindleg which was badly swollen and full of pus. It was about three inches long and the skin was just hanging open in flaps.

"It's badly infected," James said. "No wonder the poor lad doesn't look too happy. It should have been treated days ago."

"What's caused it?" I asked, trying to stay calm but feeling sick inside.

"Some kind of projection," James said. "Wire, a nail, something he's banged into which is hardly surprising in that death trap. These splinters are going to be murder to get out."

"Is he going to be all right?" Rocky said, and I suddenly remembered reading about infections and blood poisoning.

"Let's put it this way," James said. "I think we've found him in the nick of time."

It took ages for the horsebox to arrive. It was the same one that had taken Blake to Olympia but this time one of the grooms was driving. It was going to be a real trial getting Terence up the ramp. This is where our very own horse ambulance would have been a godsend.

"He's not in terrible physical condition," James

said. "He should put on weight pretty fast."

Terence looked extremely skinny but I knew that pure throughbreds tended to drop weight very quickly and some generous helpings of sugar beet and barley would soon build him up.

From what we could make out, Terence had been left some hay, although most of it was mouldy. He was desperately thirsty but James wouldn't let him drink too much at once in case it gave him colic.

"Of course, we don't know how much damage there is mentally," James said.

It was just as easy for horses to have nervous breakdowns as it was humans.

"But a few months at Hollywell should soon see him right."

We were just coaxing him up the ramp of the horsebox when a Land Rover roared into the farm-yard, slamming on the brakes and scattering hens and ducks everywhere.

I couldn't believe who got out of the driving seat. None other than Tom Richards. Of all the brazen-faced . . .

"You've ruined me," he screeched, staggering across to us. He looked as if he hadn't had a shave for days and he seemed to have aged ten years.

"You interfering, jumped-up, little twerp!" He turned on Rocky. "If you hadn't come snooping round none of this would have happened. It's all your fault."

Tom Richards shook his fist at us and James had to restrain him from taking a swing at Rocky.

"It's nobody's fault but your own," Rocky yelled back. "You've ruined yourself. Look at you, you're pathetic."

I had never seen Rocky so worked up. His neck had turned bright red and he was digging his fingers into the leadrope he was holding as if he wanted to throttle Mr Richards with it.

"Look at this horse! Look at what you did to Dancer!" Rocky shouted. "Don't you have any conscience?"

"They're just horses," Tom Richards spat out. "You lot are just out to cause trouble."

"I hope they lock you up and throw away the key," Rocky snarled.

"Now that's enough," James said, holding back Richards who was trying to lunge at Rocky. "Get out of here before we phone the police or before you get charged with assault," he continued. "Aren't you in enough trouble as it is?"

Richards saw sense and backed off towards his Land Rover.

"You won't get away with this," he threatened, as a parting shot.

"See you in court," Rocky said, with steely conviction.

"Phew," Ross said, when the Land Rover was out of sight.

A cold shiver of anger ran up my back. "He just doesn't care, does he? If Terence had been dead he wouldn't have batted an eyelid!"

"Wherever there're horses, they'll be people to abuse them," James said. "All we can do is pick up the pieces."

"It's not right though," Rocky said, and I knew how he felt. Nothing could justify cruelty to animals, especially one whose freedom we've taken away.

"Come on, old boy," Rocky said to Terence. "Let's get you home."

"They're here!" Katie shrieked, as we pulled into the yard in the horsebox.

Jigsaw was barking like mad and Sarah came running out of the house in her slippers and frantically tying her hair back with a bit of old boot lace.

"How is he?" Blake shouted from Colorado's stable where he was putting up a haynet.

"What's he like?" Katie said, as we lowered the ramp.

Danny opened the stable door next to Queenie

which was to be Terence's new home.

"It's all ready," he said proudly, and inside there wasn't a blade of straw out of place, a far cry from the terrible conditions we'd just left behind.

"He'll be OK," James said, as Terence nervously examined his new stable. "He just needs lots of loving care."

"Christmas cake, and don't forget the peanuts," Katie yelled.

"Double cream and more chocolates," James wrote down on his list which was already two feet long.

Sarah and James were going off to do the Christmas shopping. It was Christmas Eve and the only festive food we had in the house was Blake's 20lb turkey which he had won as part of his prize at Olympia. Sarah had grave reservations about getting it in the oven.

Blake was hobbling around looking decidedly pale. We had completely forgotten about his ankle at Olympia but when he got back to Hollywell he could barely walk. Sarah dragged him off to the hospital to have it X-rayed and it turned out that he'd chipped the bone just as she'd originally thought. The good news was that Mr Sullivan had been true to his word and was already making arrangements for Blake to start the New Year in his own show-jumping yard.

"Look at this," I said, opening up a Christmas card with a donkey on the front and a cheque for £30 inside.

We'd had loads of Christmas cards from supporters. One lady had even sent in half a dozen bright pink water buckets with some of the ponies' names painted on the front, and a Christmas stocking containing special horse treats, carrots and a whole new set of brushes. Also we'd made enough money from the concert to buy a horse trailer which was going to be brilliant and we'd sold out of Christmas cards and sweatshirts. Rocky was staying at Hollywell for Christmas Day but the bad news was that he had to leave for America in one week's time.

"Look, it's snowing!" Katie yelled, as thick flakes swirled down into the stable yard. Queenie's ears were already speckled with white as she looked out over her door. It had been snowing on and off since Olympia but nobody had expected it to snow for Christmas.

"Good King Wencelas looked out..." Katie started singing.

"On the feast of Stephen," I joined in.

Sarah came back from the supermarket weighed down with carrier bags and complaining that she'd nearly been mugged by an old lady for the last box of chocolate cream eggs. James was on call and he'd had to rush off to see a pregnant ewe which was having a premature birth, so Sarah had to drive Rocky's limousine back through town which had nearly killed her. Rocky had disappeared earlier that morning in our old Volvo and nobody knew where.

"What's this?" Sarah said, looking through the window and nearly dropping a packet of Christmas crackers on Jigsaw's head.

Turning into the drive, having a lot of trouble with the gears and scraping the branches of Sarah's prize holly tree was a beautiful classic Vincent horsebox.

"It's like something out of *National Velvet*," Ross said, pressing his nose against the window pane to get a better look.

"I don't believe it," Sarah shouted, craning her neck to see the driver. "It's Rocky!"

"So what do you think?" Rocky gasped, jumping out of the cab and opening the groom's door at the back. Inside it was all varnished and in immaculate condition.

We all stood in a line with snowflakes landing on our heads and our mouths dropping somewhere round our ankles.

"It . . . it's beautiful," Sarah said, as Rocky handed her the keys.

"Our very own horsebox," Katie breathed.

"I had to be quick," Rocky explained. "It was going so cheap – that's why I took the Volvo. If I'd have turned up in the limo the price would have doubled. Lucky the farmer didn't recognize me, eh?"

"It's like a dream," Sarah said in a watery voice.

Horseboxes were preferable to trailers because there was more room and horses generally travelled better in them.

"Well, don't just stand there," Rocky said. "Let's go for a test drive!"

"Merry Christmas!" Rocky shouted, careering down the stairs and nearly going head over heels on one of Jigsaw's Bonos.

It was nine o'clock on Christmas morning and we'd already been up since the crack of dawn. Katie couldn't wait to start opening the presents and was charging round the house in a jockey skull cap, complete with multi-coloured silk and chin guard. Danny was delighted with a brand-new Puffa coat and refused to take it off even though the central heating was on full blast and he was bright red in the face.

Ross insisted on taking everyone's photograph and one of the horsebox which was parked in front of the kitchen window in pride of place. He even took a sneaky one of Sarah fighting with the 20lb turkey which refused to go in the oven and she ended up with most of the stuffing all over the floor and some streaks of bacon sticking to the cupboard doors.

"Where's the mayonnaise?" James asked, wearing Sarah's frilly apron and looking exceptionally vague.

He was making a prawn cocktail sauce but he didn't seem to have a clue what he was doing.

Rocky had given us all "Rocky – The Return" leather jackets which were fantastic and he'd also given Sarah a beautiful silk shawl. We spent the morning driving round the country lanes in the horsebox with Rocky driving and us waving and tooting at everybody we knew and most of the people we didn't. Katie insisted we must have Hollywell Stables on the side and a picture of Queenie for good luck. Ross asked how much it was all going to cost.

Back at Hollywell, Sarah was panicking.

"Where is James?" she said, peeling the sprouts and trying to time the turkey which was hardly cooking at all.

Ross, Katie, Danny and Blake collapsed in front

of the television to watch the afternoon film and the Queen's speech. Rocky and I drew the short straw for feeding the horses but I didn't really mind because it was their Christmas too and they were all going to have extra carrots as a treat.

Rocky brought Queenie, Sophie and Bluey in out of the field while I fed Dancer and then put fresh straw down for Terence.

"Aren't they beautiful?" I said wistfully to Rocky as we emptied the last of the feeds into Terence's manger. He was already looking a hundred times better and was growing in confidence every day.

"They're all special," Rocky said, passing me a headcollar and leadrope. "This is what really matters, Mel, not being rich and famous, but saving lives."

"Come on, you two," Sarah yelled from the backdoor, banging on a saucepan with a wooden spoon and flushed from too much sherry.

We finally sat down for Christmas lunch at 5 o'clock in the afternoon. The turkey had taken forever to cook; the sprouts had drooped and the gravy had turned into custard slices but nobody seemed to care.

Everyone was wearing party hats, even Jigsaw who was trying to flick his off with his front paw. Oswald and Matilda were devouring a paper plate of turkey portions and outside the horses were munching into extra carrots, molasses and linseed.

"Watch out," Sarah shouted as James set the Christmas pudding on fire and the tablecloth nearly went up in flames. Rocky pulled a cracker and read out a joke about a chicken crossing the road which was as old as time itself, and Katie said she felt sick.

"Speech, speech," Rocky insisted, clinking his glass with his fork to get everyone's attention.

"Hear, hear," James mumbled, sliding further down his chair.

"I'd just like to say," Rocky said, his paper hat cocking dangerously to one side. "I'd just like to say . . ."

"Come on, get on with it," we all yelled.

"Blinkin 'eck," Rocky said, plopping down in his chair and wiping a tear from his eye. "This is the best Christmas I've ever 'ad."

Sarah kissed him on the cheek and Rocky stood up saying there was more.

"I'm writing a song about Hollywell," he said in a deadly serious voice. "And with the money we should be able to put up that stable block you're always talking about. And," he went on, "it's going to go all the way to number one!"

We sat there looking like statues in dumbfounded shock and Ross nearly choked on his cracker and cheese.

"It's too much," Sarah said, but Rocky told her to shut up and stop looking a gift horse in the mouth.

"Hollywell forever," Ross shouted as we all clinked our glasses together.

"It's the best Christmas of all time," Katie yelled.

And I couldn't have agreed more.

Hollywell Stables 1

Flying Start by Samantha Alexander

Hollywell Stables – sanctuary for horses and ponies. It was a dream come true for Mel, Ross and Katie . . .

A mysterious note led them to Queenie, neglected and desperately hungry, imprisoned in a scrapyard. Rescuing Colorado was much more complicated. The spirited Mustang terrified his wealthy owner: her solution was to have him destroyed.

But for every lucky horse at the sanctuary there are so many others in desperate need of rescue. And money is running out fast . . .

How can the sanctuary keep going?

Hollywell Stables 3

Revenge by Samantha Alexander

Hollywell Stables – sanctuary for horses and ponies. It was a dream come true for Mel, Ross and Katie . . .

Emotions run high at Hollywell stables when the local hunt comes crashing through the yard. The consequences are disastrous, and Charles Stonehouse is to blame.

Then one of the sanctuary's own ponies goes missing. Could the culprit be Bazz, who is back on the scene and out for revenge? The Hollywell team know they have to act fast: there's no time to lose . . .

Hollywell Stables 4

Fame by Samantha Alexander

Hollywell Stables – sanctuary for horses and ponies. It was a dream come true for Mel, Ross and Katie . . .

Rocky's new record, *Chase the Dream*, shoots straight into the Top Ten, and all the proceeds are going to Hollywell Stables. It brings overnight fame to the sanctuary and the family are asked to do television and radio interviews. In one show they get a call from a girl who has seen a miniature horse locked in a caravan, but rings off before telling them where it was. The Hollywell team set off to unravel the mystery . . .

All Because of Polly
by Wendy Douthwaite

At long last, Jess has her own pony – Polly, a beautiful grey Arab. Jess and her friends form a pony club and life seems perfect, until Polly gets tetanus and nearly dies. As Jess and her family fight for Polly's life, they have no idea what the pony's recovery will mean. For Jess it is a happy ending, but for her friend Beckie, confined to a wheelchair after a car crash, the consequences are far more than that – for her it is the most important thing that ever could have happened . . .

Polly on Location
by Wendy Douthwaite

"We think we'll need some extras, sometime next week," he explained. "Some riders and ponies. It will be for a night-time scene. Smugglers coming back from the coast, some riding, some leading pack-horses that sort of thing. And we could do with some horse help, today, too. Interested?"

When Jessica Caswell suggests to her friends in the Edgecombe Valley Riding Club that they audition for the filming, she never dreamt that she and her beautiful Arab mare, Polly, would play the star role!

Other People's Ponies
by Wendy Douthwaite

It seemed to Jess that she would never have a pony of her own. All she ever did was look after other people's ponies. First there was Beetle, then the plump and lazy Muffin and finally there was Polly, a beautiful grey Arab mare, who was her dream pony made real. If only dreams could be made real, too!

'Polished sensitive writing about feelings and friendships which develops into an unexpected and bitter-sweet ending.'
Books For Keeps